PRAISE FOR STEPHEN MERTZ

"Stephen Mertz is a Grandmaster of action/adventure!"
—*MensAdventureMagazine&Books.com*

"Hard-edged! For those who like their tales straight and sharp!"
—Joe R. Lansdale

*"Stephen Mertz is the best action writer I've read in a long time...
the Cody's War series is filled with everything you want from a
master writer!"*
—Brent Towns, bestselling author of the Team Reaper series

"Action-driven!"
—*Publisher's Weekly*

"The cleanest, strongest prose in the business!"
—*Gravetapping.com*

"One of the best writers in the genre!"
—Max Allan Collins

"One of the genre's best storytellers!
—*Paperback Warrior*

*"Stephen Mertz's latest Cody's War novel demonstrates that he
hasn't lost a step and is still a legend in the action/adventure
field. One of the best adventure writers of our time!"*
—James M. Reasoner, *New York Times* bestselling author

HELLFIRE IN SYRIA

CODY'S WAR BOOK TEN

STEPHEN MERTZ

*ROUGH
EDGES
PRESS*

**ROUGH
EDGES
PRESS**

Published in the United States by Wolfpack Publishing, Las Vegas
Rough Edges Press
An Imprint of Wolfpack Publishing
9850 S. Maryland Parkway, Suite A-5 #323
Las Vegas, Nevada 89183

roughedgespress.com

Paperback ISBN 978-1-68549-292-2
eBook ISBN 978-1-68549-291-5
LCCN 2023936145

HELLFIRE IN SYRIA

For Mike Bray
Publisher. Visionary. Friend.

CHAPTER ONE

Rome—0700 hours

Abdul Kemal checked the accuracy of his wristwatch against the wall clock behind the standup counter of the snack bar that was busy with the shoulder-to-shoulder press of office workers stopping off for a quick cup of coffee and pastry on their way to work.

He finished his orange juice in a quick gulp and left the little *tavola calda*, emerging onto Via Vittorio Veneto in a steady downpour that made this new day grim and humid. The wide thoroughfare practically overflowed with bumper-to-bumper traffic whizzing by dangerously fast in either direction.

He clenched his teeth against the relentless car horns sounding amid the traffic, incessantly beeping at each other, underscored by the sibilant hiss of tires on wet pavement.

A Volvo glided out from the speeding flow of traffic and pulled to the curb, its back door yawning open before the car came to a full stop.

Kemal held back only a moment, his fingertips poised near the front of his open jacket, near the automatic pistol he wore holstered beneath the jacket. Then he recognized one of the two men inside the Volvo in the gloomy daylight that was more night than day because of the low, dark rain clouds. He climbed into the backseat, finding the car's interior uncomfortable and muggy, almost claustrophobic. He was used to the open spaces of the desert.

The Volvo eased back into the traffic with the same seemingly effortless ease the driver had exhibited in pulling up to the curb.

"You have lost none of your vehicular skills since the last time, I see, Majid," Kemal said to the back of the driver's head.

Majid Baqir caught Kemal's eyes in the rearview mirror and chuckled without humor.

"I have gotten better, if anything, Abdul. Damascus was good for not much else, I'm sad to say. It is good to see you again, old friend."

Kemal's gaze shifted to the passenger in the front seat.

"You are Fared al-Hor. You have something for me."

The other man turned halfway around in the front seat and cleared his throat, extending a cloth backpack over the back of the car seat.

"I am most honored to be working with the great Abdul Kemal, the most effective operative of all those who serve Hezbollah."

Kemal took the backpack, lowering it beside him to the seat, well below window level. He unzipped the pack and reached inside.

"Only Allah is great. We are but the instruments of his divine will."

He extracted one of the compact, lightweight Uzi submachine guns which the backpack contained, withdrawing a handful of 32-round magazines and dropping them into the pocket of his jacket except for palming one of them into the Uzi's pistol grip.

The *snick-snack* of the Volvo's windshield wipers filled the car's interior.

"This rain," said Majid to Kemal's reflection in the rearview, "do you think it will cause problems?"

Kemal's eyes lifted from the Uzi to look out through the rivulet-streaked windshield.

"Problems? No, not for us. For those we have come for, yes. We have the element surprise, and the rain will be our ally."

He thought that he could have added that they would need all the allies they could get, making an assault, as they were about to, on a private residence that had been converted into a CIA "safe house" in middle of this fashionable Rome neighborhood. But Kemal told himself that these two would hardly need to be reminded of the realities of their mission. Kemal and Majid had worked together before on exactly this sort of operation. Majid was an enforcer, a skillful killer, and the best fast-car driver, especially in a combat situation, that Kemal had ever worked with. Fared al-Hor was their Syrian contact. On occasion, Iran lends out the services of Hezbollah if there is a mutual interest in the result. This time it was the Syrians. Fared was command level, his role being to supply and fund the operation.

"Allah's will be done," Majid intoned solemnly.

The three of them lapsed into silence.

Kemal closed his eyes and, with his finger curled around the Uzi's trigger, he went over the plan step by step one more time, but he could find no last minute corrections to be made. In going over the plan, he found himself thinking again of how far his destiny had brought him to this point in time, to this place and what was about to happen. He realized once again that for him there could be no other life.

He had been born in Lebanon. A child when the Zionist warmongers had invaded, he'd witnessed the death of his mother and father during a shelling of Beirut. In that war-torn hell on earth he, his brothers and sisters—all of them mere children—had been spirited away by relatives to some filthy refugee camp. His two older brothers had died fighting the Jews. His sister lost her life in a refugee camp in Beirut.

Allah's will alone could only be responsible for Kemal's survival and for over the years following his path to find a life in Iran where his inner demons could be satisfied by action. His hatred of the Zionists and their American cohorts fueled his rage and commitment to a never-ending holy war. War, yes. Holy War. *Jihad.*

The enemy called it "acts of terrorism."

Innocent lives among the enemy lost? Those lives were no more innocent than the lives of Kemal's mother, father, brothers, and sister to his way of thinking. The tears he had shed for them had been, and would be, exchanged for blood until the day he died. He would die fighting the enemies of his people. If not today, then someday. It could be no other way. He would have it no different, for then he would be reunited with his family in paradise, graced with Allah's favor forevermore.

Kemal had insisted on being in on this operation. His reputation in Hezbollah was that of one who did far more than simply plan the missions, and then sit back while others took the risks. He went into the fires of battle with his brothers in Hezbollah.

His notoriety among allies and enemies alike stemmed from his genius for planning and executing flawless operations, capturing headlines time and again. He was known to be the planner of a massacre in a Jewish restaurant in Paris seven months ago. An attempted assassination of the Israeli ambassador in London had been aborted at the last moment when the ambassador's plans had changed too late for Kemal to redeploy his assets. A month ago, he had been spotted in the vicinity only moments before a bomb blast had torn apart a Rome shopping mall, leaving twelve dead.

A devious route had brought him to Rome this time after his briefing in Tehran. He had organized the movement and timetables for his small team, arranging for them to arrive in Rome independently of each other over the past two days. Fared had relinquished command of this morning's hit in recognition of Kemal's reputation and skill set. The Syrians were supplying the money and the weapons but Fared, like Majid, would follow Kemal's orders in their roles in the upcoming action.

Kemal felt his pulse pound in anticipation of what was about to happen. He'd labored many hours over the plan and had made several visits, walking past the safe house, photographing the house and its immediate surroundings from as many angles as possible.

Cars were parked bumper to bumper along the busy thoroughfare that ran past the safe house, an anonymous one-level structure located mid-block in a row of similar residences. Not more than a dozen blocks from the US Embassy.

Across the street at the opposite end of the block from the house, a vehicle was just pulling away from the curb. Majid effortlessly steered the Volvo into the vacated space, aligning with the curb. He switched off the ignition.

Kemal handed each of them an Uzi, ammunition and ordinance.

He said, "It is the moment of truth. Good luck, my brothers."

Majid said, "May Allah be with us."

Fared said nothing.

There was nothing more to say. They had gone over this often enough for them to function together like a smooth running machine. They left the Volvo, each man hiding his compact weapon beneath his jacket.

They waited briefly for a break in the traffic, then crossed the rain-swept street, joining an unending stream of umbrella wielding pedestrians clogged the sidewalks. The army of day workers on their way to another day at the office or shop, crowding the sidewalks against a backdrop of a somehow orderly melee of cars, trucks, and Rome's great green buses racing past. To anyone watching cameras that may have been placed around the safe house for security purposes, the three of them appeared to be nothing more than three ordinary-looking fellows hunched against the elements as they made their way along the crowded sidewalk.

It was only when they were a handful of paces from the safe house property line that the next phase of the hit was initiated. Moving with an absolute economy of movement but without appearing to hurry, they split up at the mouth of a narrow walkway that ran between the safe house and the identical structure next door. Kemal strode briskly down the walkway that offered little shelter from the light rain. Previous reconnoitering had revealed the safe house's back door. Majid and Fared stepped up to the front door of the house so quickly there was no time for reaction of any sort from within even if did have a security camera setup.

Each man reached into a pocket without slackening their pace, yanking out grenades. Majid and Fared pulled the pins and tossed their grenades at the front door, quickly drawing back behind the corner of the building for protection. The grenades detonated, blowing aside several passersby in a bloodied explosion of violence on this normal everyday street. With the hellish roar still rumbling, the pair of terrorists revealed their submachine guns and charged the gutted front entrance of a house no longer safe.

Despite his extensive planning, Kemal ran into the unexpected when he rounded the rear of the house. Unlike his previous visits, this time there was a man in civilian attire, holding an assault rifle, standing at the rear entrance.

Kemal revealed himself to the man only after he'd pulled the pin of his grenade. He tossed the grenade before the man in the closed doorway could track up the assault rifle he held. The guard saw the grenade land between his feet too late to do anything but open his mouth to shout a warning to those inside. Too late. The grenade detonated, exploding shrapnel that whisked the man off his feet, hurling his body to the ground like a straw man tossed in a violent windstorm.

In the front half of the house, three sleepy-eyed CIA agents clad in casual civilian wear, armed with submachine guns, flew into response mode as Majid and Fared stormed in through the wreckage of the blown-out front door. Two of the agents, a man and a woman, had been sitting on kitchen chairs tilted back against the wall, sipping coffee, weapons straddling their laps. The third, a man off to their side, had been sitting on a sofa monitoring the street camera but who hadn't had time to react before two normal looking fellows on the rainy sidewalk hurled their grenades.

These agents were trained professionals. But Kemal understood their mindset. They thought because they'd made it through another night without incident that they could relax, if not let down their guard and enjoy their coffee and some early morning chit chat, not expecting a swift, maximum hard strike to come down on them at this hour.

The two seated agents righted their chairs simultaneously and jumped up, tracking their weapons around. The man on the sofa actually got his weapon swung all the way around into firing position from where he jarred himself erect from the sofa. He squeezed off a short, nasty, silenced burst.

Majid and Fared saw it coming and fell forward as soon as they cleared the door, Majid coming through first, Fared right behind him. Each man hit his belly to a wooden floor, projectiles razoring the air just above where their bodies had been a millisecond before. They skidded along the wood slightly, each man bringing his weapon around to home in on targets, aiming with their elbows placed on the floor.

Fared triggered a burst of lead that pumped one of the male agents with a chest level sweep of .45-caliber bullets packing enough force to lift him off his feet, pitching his riddled body through a doorway directly behind him.

Kemal opened up on the female agent who was in the process of bringing her weapon to bear on them. His Uzi stuttered flame. The woman caught a line of lead stitching across her chest before she could fire, projectiles pitching her into a corner of the breakfast nook, upending the table in the process.

The acrid bite of hazing gunsmoke hung heavy in the air.

Kemal and Fared leapt to their feet, slapping fresh magazines into their weapons. A violent racket erupted from the back of the house.

They hurried in that direction.

CHAPTER TWO

In the exploding fragmentation of her reality, overwhelmed by sudden and total violence, Denise Rashid experienced a pocket of lucidity.

No one was safe.

Your world can explode in a heartbeat.

One heartbeat earlier, Denise had been sitting in her reading chair, enjoying a good book that was taking her mind off her troubles. She was enjoying the patter of rain on the sitting room window, comfortable with her 10-year-old son, Ali, who'd been playing a game on his tablet across the room. They were safe and secure with the CIA people just beyond a closed door that afforded her and Ali a degree of privacy while another armed sentry stood guard on the other side of the outside door.

The past week had been life-changing and tumultuous beyond belief, but until a heartbeat ago it had felt good to be in Rome again, a dozen years since her last visit. At that time, she'd managed to attract a future husband at a Middle East oil consortium conference in Dubai. She was chief assistant to the

CEO of an American firm being represented at the conference.

She and Ahmed had taken to each other socially. Her soon-to-be husband was a handsome, erudite, empathetic man who had gone about courting her with style and elegance. Denise's friends told her she was crazy.

But that was a dozen years ago.

It hadn't been all that easy at first. She had given up her former life as an everyday kid from Indianapolis, her adult life as a liberated, successful woman in the global business world. Her life became a different culture, a different religion. But love had seen them through; her and Ahmed.

An ugly civil war raged in her new country but Ahmed's wealth and government position allowed her to live in a luxurious bubble. Ahmed became affiliated with the Syrian government and introduced her to a life of luxury and experience. They traveled throughout Europe, Asia and the Middle East before Ali was born. With a loving husband and a son to raise, it was a good life.

That is until her husband took his stand.

Their little family had to flee for their lives. Leave everything behind. But the same sense of adventure that had originally allowed her to embrace life in Syria had also brought her onboard with Ahmed's decision to defect to the west. She thought she'd understood the risks they were taking, but their lives during this past week, since their arrival in Rome, had enlightened her to the true level of risk undertaken by their defection.

Rome was as beautiful as she remembered it to be. She even loved the cacophony of its ceaseless traffic. A safe house run by America's Central Intelligence Agency. Bodyguards. The agents assigned to guard the family made up a nice crew. Denise enjoyed overhearing the American slang that passed between them, it had taken on a whole new set of words and phrases. The woman agent was good company whenever a chance to visit came up. Still, Denise's life in seclusion since coming to Rome had been more restricted than the life she'd left behind.

Ahmed was presently at the American Embassy, attending another early morning briefing as the Rashid family was processed through a system that would eventually, she was told, see them to a safe life in America.

And that's when the world exploded.

An Arab male with a machine gun kicked open the shattered outside doorway and came storming in.

Denise's maternal instinct kicked in reflexively, without thought. She flung herself toward Ali. Her son looked dazed, his hands to his head, his eyes wide. In those heartbeats before she could reach him across that short distance, the Arab had shoulder-slung his weapon and was upon her, not giving her even the chance to cry out. Another Arab rushed into the sitting room from the front of the house. This one scooped up little Ali.

It happened so fast.

Denise tried to struggle but the Arab holding her easily overpowered and physically restrained her. Her little boy was too dazed to even put up a fight. They rushed her and Ali through the house and out into the street. Outside, pedestrians were crouched behind whatever cover was available in the rain, observing with stunned eyes and gaping jaws an incident unfolding in no more than a minute.

Another Arab male sat behind the steering wheel of an idling Volvo. Denise and Ali were roughly tossed into the waiting vehicle. One of the men followed them into the rear seat, the other threw himself into the front passenger side. The doors slammed shut. The driver punched the accelerator. The car leapt away.

On a lesser traveled side street, the Volvo merged with the traffic flow. Denise continued to struggle, twisting frantically in the confines of the back seat. She cried out at the man crowding her and Ali.

"Who are you? Let us out of here! Let me—"

Kemal punched her sharply in the jaw.

Denise's eyes rolled back in their sockets. She crumpled into the narrow space on the floor. The last thing she heard before losing consciousness was the anguished shout of her son.

The Volvo tooled along. It was hot and stuffy in the car. Ali crouched in the far corner, frightened eyes transfixed on his unconscious mother.

The driver chuckled from behind the steering wheel.

"She has spirit, this one!"

Kemal gazed down at the woman's still form. He massaged his knuckles.

"It will not be easy for these two."

Fared added, without a trace of sincerity, "I almost feel sorry for them."

CHAPTER THREE

Summers was the CIA control officer conducting Ahmed Rashid's debriefing. A compact, intense man in his thirties, he had ordered his staff not to interrupt the briefing with Rashid under any circumstance. That's how important his defection was.

So when a clerical assistant did intrude, handing a cell phone to Summers with whispered words of urgency, a warning impulse registered within Ahmed Rashid. This could only be something most serious.

Summers took the call without saying a word. He listened, and then disconnected within less than a minute. He returned the cell to his assistant who withdrew from the briefing room. The CIA man's normal intense, all-business demeanor had clouded with an emotion Rashid recognized as concern.

Knowing the answer, Rashid said, "It is bad news, Mr. Summers?"

Summers rose to his feet, his take care of business demeanor back in place. "Please come with me. I'll tell you what happened on the way."

Less than twenty minutes later, the two men stood in the front room of the busy scene in the house where four body bags were lined up on the floor. Everything in sight was in shambles: bullet-riddled furniture and walls with splashes of blood glistening everywhere.

Ahmed Rashid was in a state of shock and outrage.

During the chauffeured drive that had brought them the short distance to this awful scene of carnage, Summers had delivered a concise report of what he'd been informed had happened. Summers' remarks had been concise and brief since he himself had little to go on at this point. He spent most of the trip with his cell phone pressed to his ear, making only monosyllabic grunts as he listened to the flow of developing information.

The shock and anger Rashid felt was mirrored in Summers' expression as they stood in the front room taking stock. First responders were packing up to leave while newly arrived forensics specialists had already begun the process of minute examination, taking measurements, taking photographs.

Rashid found his voice. "How can such a thing be? My Denise and little Ali..." A note of accusation crept into his words. "Mr. Summers, you assured me they would be safe while I was away. Now...where are they?"

Summers said, "At least we know they're alive or they'd have been left behind, too." He indicated the body bags to make his point. "You have my sympathy, sir. The agency won't rest until whoever did this has been brought to justice."

"Justice? Do not speak to me of legal concepts at this point, agent. Your people are dead. My wife and child are missing. How could this have happened?"

"Training," said Summers. "From what little we have so far, it's obvious this was a well-coordinated hit executed by a highly trained top-flight unit. No other way it could have happened. No excuses. That's the bottom line. And when I say justice, Mr. Rashid, I'm talking about settling a blood debt." Summers' eyes made another scan of the lined-up body bags. Another trace of emotion. "I knew every one of these people personally. Good, decent human beings. Damn it to hell."

Inside, Rashid fought to resist the despair that was trying to claim him along with the shock and the knowledge of what happened here.

Violence. Death.

This is what he had so wanted to avoid; why he fled, defecting from the land of his birth. But death and violence had followed him. He didn't want his son to grow up in a culture of war and violence. He'd been part of the government, that was true. It was also true that his revulsion to what his life had become had grown so great that in the interests of his family and his own peace of mind and perhaps his country's future he had seen no other course open to him but to defect.

He had done so only after secretly compiling an extensive document composed of everything from official interagency memos and emails to actual photographs of the aftermath of hideous war crimes: mass civilian executions, use of poison gas to wipe out entire communities—that sort of thing. Documentation of a decade of atrocities committed by the Syrian government away from the eyes of the civilized world.

That was why it mattered so much to the regime in Damascus.

And now, *this...*

Rashid asked, "What is your next course of action, Agent Summers?"

He'd seen little choice but to share with Summers the phone message he'd received on his cell minutes earlier while the agent had first been busy gaining them official entry through the outer cordon of city police who had been directed to seal off the area. Not recognizing the incoming number, Rashid had taken the call. The message had been spoken without inflection, the words themselves ominous enough.

"We have your wife and son. Return home."

Nothing more. The caller disconnected, the call likely made from a prepaid cell now residing in a dumpster somewhere.

During his days of meetings with Summers at the embassy, Rashid had taken the CIA man's measure. Rashid's time in the oil business had placed him in regular contact with American men. He knew and respected the breed. Men of direct action. Summers measured up.

He made direct eye contact with Rashid so there would be no mistaking his sincerity. He said, "Syria is behind this, of course. They expect us to come up with a cover story for the carnage here and to keep your defection under cover and away from the media. They don't want the world to know about any of this. I'd say this was the work of Iranians paid by the Syrians. It's how they usually work it over there. I intend to work every asset and lead we have to clarify and neutralize the situation."

"By neutralize I assume you mean locate and rescue my wife

and child, yes?"

"That is precisely what I mean," said Summers. "But speaking man to man, Rashid, I'd say the real question now is what is *your* intended course of action?"

Rashid's response came only after a lengthy pause.

"That is a decision with only one answer. Are you a married man, agent? Do you have a family?"

"I do."

"Then if you were me, what would you do?"

"You're right," said Summers, maintaining that direct eye contact. "There is only one answer to a choice like that. The information you're sharing in cooperating with us is the prevention of untold future atrocities. But you're being asked to balance that against the lives of your wife and child."

"Thank you for understanding."

Summers again indicated the carnage around them.

"But this isn't endgame," he said. "We can move fast when we have to. Those phone calls I took on our way over...something this big has to make a ripple. There's a chance intel coming in now may develop into something. That's what we're going on anyway."

"That at least is some good news," said Rashid. "But with the lives of my family at stake...I just don't know what to do."

"I can only sympathize with you," said Summers, "and assure you that we're moving full speed on this. I'm told our best man is on it."

CHAPTER FOUR

Damascus—Seven hours later

Jack Cody smelled an ambush. But he and Sara had come too far. There was no turning back now.

Damascus is the oldest city in the world, continuously inhabited since the third millennium BC. Located in Southwestern Syria, 50 miles inland from the eastern shore of the Mediterranean, Damascus today is the center of a large metropolitan area with a population of over three million people.

The Old City of Damascus is surrounded by its original ancient ramparts. Many buildings have been abandoned or are falling into disrepair, sometimes standing side by side with upscale structures like *Beit al-Mamlouka*, a 17th-Century building serving as a luxury boutique hotel within the Old City these days.

That site was several blocks away from the position where Cody and Sara now stood in the shadows, waiting.

This part of the Old City was a dreary, abandoned neighborhood of narrow streets, deep shadows and distant echoes; some of those echoes urban, others stirred as if by ancient memory. It was a foreboding place of mysterious shadow under a quarter moon.

Cody and Sara had been in the country less than an hour. They were here to make contact with a civilian asset, their first step in this mission to rescue a pair of hostages taken in Rome. Intel developed thus far indicated Denise Rashid and her son were being held at an as yet unspecified location in Iraq along the Syrian-Iraqi border. Their exact location was likely to be developed at any moment, at least, according to what Cody and Sara had been told before their insertion into Syria. Neighboring Iraq was chosen by the kidnappers to provide the Syrian government, which had planned and financed the kidnapping, with plausible deniability.

Rival Shiite groups have been deadlocked in Iraq forming a government ever since Desert Storm and would have had no tolerance for another US military incursion. Thus, this mission had been handed to Cody. His recent mission in Afghanistan already had him and Sara Durell in the region.

Sara was along due to both her skillset as a field operative—which matched Cody's—and because she had insisted, feeling her presence as a woman could aid in dealing with the woman and child when they were located and freed.

With the clock chipping away at the 72-hour deadline the terrorists had given Ahmed, time was of the essence.

Cody and Sara were dressed in civilian black, blending

seamlessly with the gathering gloom of oncoming night. Both held a small backpack packed with compact weaponry and munitions.

They were in a high danger zone in one of the world's most dangerous cities. The air was heavy with heat, humidity, pollution and a clammy atmosphere of collective human fear and paranoia of a metropolis existing on the edge of chaos and collapse.

Syria today was a devastated country with the world's largest refugee crisis. With a collapsed economy, there were shortages of fuel and electricity. More than half of the country's people were displaced. Two-thirds of those displaced being women and children. More than eighty percent of the population continues to live in poverty.

The situation was beyond horrible. Healthcare centers and hospitals, schools, utilities, and water and sanitation systems were damaged or destroyed, and busy marketplaces have been reduced to rubble. Along the frontier, many who fought for the regime have become warlords who now control their own fiefdoms, semi-independent of Damascus. Syria was a tattered nation unable to hide the ravages of twelve years of brutal civil war.

Activity from Cody's far left periphery drew his attention.

A four-year-old Fiat sedan, with only amber parking lights on, had turned onto the street two blocks away. The car advanced at an extremely cautious, slow rate of speed, advancing along the two block kill zone.

Sara commented in a whisper, "Here she comes." She and

Cody were not only combat partners. They had on occasion been lovers. She added in the first gentle tone she'd used in days, "Good luck, soldier. Ready to rock, babe?"

Cody's complete, narrow eyed focus was tracking nothing but those advancing Amber parking lights.

Cody said, "I was born ready."

* * * * *

Aisha Hassan tried to calm the fear wreaking havoc in her stomach. But she failed miserably. She had never done anything like this before.

She was 18 years old and should have been at her parents' home, studying for her upcoming exam at the University. Instead, she was easing this little sedan car along a dark, dangerous street. A part of her wanted to floor the accelerator and speed away from here altogether.

But of course that would never do.

She could not betray Aboo and the others.

Aisha's father was a ranking member of the Syrian energy department in Damascus. She had been born and raised in the luxury of the ruling class. The civil war raging beyond the walls of her protected domain had little effect on Aisha's growing years.

That is, until she enrolled in the University and met a handsome lad of nearly identical age, class and upbringing. She and Aboo had fallen in love; teenagers in a global reality whether their parents or government approved or not.

Like many their age, Aisha and Aboo secretly listened to American rock and roll and read books forbidden under Islamic law in a sort of teenage cultural underground that exists in most hardcore Islamic countries in the region.

It had been an exciting time for Aisha and soon she found herself becoming involved in Aboo's politics along with his friends. In the subtlest, and she often thought inconsequential, ways their little teenage social group had gone about taking on a sense of solidarity with the very rebels who were fighting throughout the country to overthrow the government.

That was a year ago.

Tonight she was carrying out a mission assigned to her by Aboo's superior. This was not her car she was driving. The GPS had been formatted. She was only to meet two Americans, a man and a woman, and turn the vehicle over to them.

Aisha had been chosen for this task because, on the surface, she seemed to have nothing whatever to do with such a political movement. Although she had not volunteered, she had enthusiastic accepted the assignment in spite of Aboo assuring her she didn't have to unless she really wanted to become involved.

At first tonight had seemed like an adventure, a romantic adventure to please and impress Aboo, whom she was convinced was the love of her life. But now, alone in the dark, driving down this forbidding street, she was having second thoughts, worries, and the tightening of fear in her stomach muscles would not recede.

Then she saw them.

Barely discernible in the gloom, a man and woman emerged

from the shadows to stand there at the curb, waiting for her. Good, Aisha told herself with a deep sigh of relief. Everything was going as it should. Soon she would be gone from here and safe.

CHAPTER FIVE

Aisha left the key in the ignition with the car running on idle. She stepped from the vehicle.

Cody checked out her appearance. What he saw was slimming and stylish. Not a threat.

The shadowy presence of the man and woman materialized to become identifiable to Aisha in the amber glow of the car's parking lights.

The reassurance Aisha had first experienced upon seeing them now only grew warmer as they stepped forward to greet her. This was a man and woman who moved in coordination with the other with an economy of movement that reminded Aisha of some jungle animal, the panther perhaps, gracefully one with its environment and yet it's every sense primed for danger with every step.

The man had a powerful in shape physique. Thick in the shoulders. Thick dark hair with gray. A squared jaw. Piercing eyes.

The woman possessed a human warmth that shone through her animal grace. She smiled pleasantly.

"Aisha?"

Aisha nodded at the introduction. *Yes!* she told herself yet again. Everything was going to be all right.

She said, "Hello. I—"

And that was as far as she got. Aisha never said another word.

With a startled gasp, Aisha sent a wild, frightened glance over her shoulder where high voltage headlights flared to life a half-block away, dissolving the darkness behind her. Despite all of the instructions and precautions, she had been followed and not by anyone who meant her any good.

The headlight beams threw into sharp silvery relief the three of them standing there beside the idling car.

A vehicle, a panel van, lights off, sporting the insignia of the Syrian Secret Police, had screeched to a stop. The Secret Police was a government death squad feared throughout the country by both sides of the Civil War, commonly known for brutality and torture.

A side door of the van popped open. A pair of commando-like figures jumped out, armed with rifles. They opened fire. The distinctive hammering of Russian-made AK47s on auto fire tore apart the night, the weapons' muzzle flashes flaring in the night like crazy strobe lights.

Cody and Sara had already flared into reflexive response, each hitting a combat crouch while unslinging and reaching into their backpacks, bringing out a mini MAC-10 submachine gun. Cody and Sara triggered withering return fire downrange at their assailants.

That's when a tight figure eight of incoming fire from the Syrians stitched a pulverizing line of bullet holes across Aisha's torso, spinning the girl around into the red rain mist from her exit wounds. The girl was flung violently against the car, and then she pitched to the ground.

Sara was able to catch Aisha's falling body, to cradle it in the strong grip of her left arm while still firing off an extended burst from the MAC-10 held in her right fist.

It was one hell of a wild shootout.

The Syrian Secret Police had not expected return fire. Silhouetted by light from inside the van, two of them became easy targets. Cody squeezed off rounds. His bullets hit both targets. One took a head hit that knocked him off his feet and back into the van. The other guy caught his in the gut. Holding onto his rifle, he doubled up, toppling to the ground.

The van squealed its tires getting away, kicking up a cloud of burnt rubber in a hurried withdrawal.

Cody rushed to the fallen gunmen. The inky human figure curled up on the ground was moaning in mortal pain, lying there in a fetal ball with a spreading pool beneath him that was black and shiny like an oil slick. Cody snatched up the AK47, prying it loose without effort from unresisting hands.

He raised the AK47 to sight in on the fleeing the van. The vehicle was fast approaching a narrow side street. Cody triggered an extended burst of auto fire that dotted a pattern across the rear of the van seconds before it gained the intersection.

The van wobbled crazily, slacking its speed but still traveling with plenty of momentum. Then it plowed into the jutting corner of a towering brick structure. There came the thudding impact of crushing metal, the shattering of glass. The gas tank exploded. The van disappeared in a bursting fireball that sent debris clattering to the nearby pavement.

Cody lowered the AK47.

The man at his feet had stopped gasping in pain. He was dead. Retaining his grip on the AK47, Cody hurried over to where Sara was releasing her hold on Aisha, stretching the dead girl out upon the pavement with the delicate touch of a natural caregiver. Traces of the girl's blood glistened on Sara's hands.

Cody, observing this, said, "Poor kid. She should've stayed home. Did she say anything?"

Never releasing the trigger finger of her right hand, filled with the machine gun pistol, Sara was able to use the thumbs of her left hand to close the lids of the dead woman's eyes widened with the pain and surprise of an unspeakably violent death.

Sara said, "She said, tell Aboo I love him."

Cody heard the sadness of a teardrop in Sara's voice but there was no trace of emotion on the combat-hard warrior mask of her features.

She cast a look downrange at the flaming remains of the Syrian van. "We need to keep moving. Those trigger boys had to be in radio contact. Whoever sent them will be sending more."

Cody drew his attention from the slaughtered innocent who'd paid with her life for having been aligned with the rebel

Free Syrian Army. Aisha had been their vital link to a civilian helicopter presently awaiting them in an outlying suburb of Damascus. From there, Cody and Sara were to be flown the 250-miles from Damascus to Deir ez-Zour, a barren, hostile, oil-rich desert province bordering Iraq...the general vicinity to which intel had thus far tracked the hostages.

Yes, Aisha Hassan should have stayed home. But no, she'd chosen instead to put herself in harm's way in a seemingly endless, hopeless civil war. And so, she had paid the ultimate price.

This was a debt Cody intended to settle in blood.

He leaned into the vehicle, automating the GPS. He said, "Destination already locked in. Let's make tracks."

Cody and Sara flung themselves into the car without further hesitation, Cody positioning himself behind the steering wheel. He handed the AK47, ungainly in the confines of the car, over to Sara who was still settling in when he floored the accelerator.

The Fiat had obviously been modified. The engine under its hood packed a punch. The momentum of the quick pick-up-and-go flung Sara forcefully against the passenger seat, her side door slamming shut under the powerful forward momentum.

This was no time for caution. Cody flicked on the headlight beams to guide them away from there.

For a short while they encountered no traffic whatsoever. Following the GPS instructions, they raced down narrow dark streets without respect for stop signs or anything else.

The streets of Damascus were practically untraveled even at this early hour of the evening. Few in the city privately owned an automobile and, if one did, there were few safe places to go despite the government's claims of law and order being restored within the capital.

Leaving the Old City at such a high rate of speed was like shedding history that flew by as if observed from a time machine. The Old City's labyrinth of ancient thoroughfares, mosques and restored tourist sites and shops peeled away first into a run of sterile, modern Western-style office complexes, modern architecture interspersed here and there with tourist oriented restaurants and stores, all of it dark and shut down.

From there they did encounter the occasional taxi cab or random delivery truck making its rounds as they sped along broad landscaped boulevards, racing through an urban landscape that soon became residential. Apartment buildings and domed mosques were interspersed with poplar trees domed mosques. Tall, slim minarets pushing skyward. This soon yielded to the less populated, more upscale outer suburbs of the city; guard gated communities and walled estates.

They almost made it to their destination.

Almost...

They picked up the first Secret Police vehicle, its siren whining full open and rooftop lights flashing, when they were less than a quarter mile from their destination according to the GPS. That first vehicle was quickly joined by a second twin Secret Police vehicle that angled in at high speed from another point, pursuit obviously being orchestrated by radio with the possible assistance of an observing chopper or a drone positioned high overhead in the night sky.

A helicopter was idling on the ground inside a fenced enclosure; a remote warehouse complex, its gate yawning open according to plan.

Cody palmed the little car's steering wheel into a screeching, two-wheel turn onto the grounds at full speed, eating up that last quarter mile of ground toward where the chopper sat warming up.

The Secret Police vehicles were closing in fast from behind, hot on Cody's ass, their rooftop lights nearly blinding as they closed in. The sirens were deafening. Cody saw in his rearview mirrors that the pursuit vehicles were bristling with gunmen leaning out their side windows for a good shot.

Cody glanced sideways at Sara. "Up for game of chicken?"

Sara checked the load and action of the AK47.

She snarled, "Bring it on!"

Without slacking even a mile off their high speed, he wheeled the small sedan around in a rubber-shredding one-hundred-and-eighty-degree turn. Drawing on all the skill of a Hollywood movie stunt driver, he brought their little sedan straight into a full-speed, full-on course that would bring them head to head with the oncoming lead pursuit vehicle.

For the first few seconds, the Syrian driver was too startled to react. Then it was too late.

Sara tracked the rifle up, aiming it out her open side window like an extended snout from their speeding vehicle. Resting her shoulder in the window frame, she carefully squeezed off three rounds, riding the rifle's recoil to place those rounds squarely into the Syrian driver's windshield, exploding the glass and the skull of the man behind the steering wheel. The unmanned vehicle swerved into a triple roll.

Audible cries from the noisy carnage came as the men inside were flung around the tumbling vehicle, only to be crushed by its weight.

The second Secret Police vehicle went rocketing past, going in the opposite direction. Cody applied some braking to make another turn, allowing Sara to pull off several rounds at the second Syrian vehicle. Its driver obviously wanted no part of the fight and was maneuvering into a tactical withdrawal. Sara held her fire.

Cody drove on to where a young Syrian male in civilian clothes stood beside the helo. He wore radio control headphones. The pilot. He stood holding open the helicopter's side hatch door in anticipation of their arrival.

Cody brought the car to a jolting stop. He and Sara ran to meet the young man.

The guy said, "I am Aboo." He eyed their car with a frown, surprised to note with growing concern that these two passengers were alone, unaccompanied. He started to say, "Where is—?"

He was interrupted by activity on the field behind them.

Another pair of Secret Police vehicles, their lights and sirens also running wide open, had entered the field. Emboldened, all three of the Syrian death squad vehicles were starting to advance.

Sara returned the AK47 to Cody. He blazed away with an extended burst at the vehicles. The Syrians slowed down but they did not stop advancing.

Sara's fingertips touched the kid's sleeve.

"Aboo," she said, "we have bad news."

Cody said, "First things first, son. Get us the hell out of Damascus."

"Yes, sir," snapped Aboo.

It was an automatic, crisp response that earned Cody's admiration. This young man knew what the bad news was, yeah. There would be mourning and tears for a lost love. But not now. Now he took control of the small chopper with cool professionalism.

The privately owned little helicopter lifted off, already well beyond range of the ground force firing ineffectively after it more for show than anything else.

Then they were on their way.

Next stop: Deir ez-Zour Province.

CHAPTER SIX

Denise Rashid came awake, startled from a fitful yet deep, dreamless sleep with a mighty gasp for air like a swimmer having been submerged underwater for too long before finally bursting to the surface.

A man was in bed with her; coarse, cursing in heat, lust, frustration.

Upon arriving at their destination inside Iraq, her capturers had provided her with a shapeless frock that buttoned down the front. Now, an unshaven brute was pawing at her, pinning her to the sheets with his weight, using both clumsy, unwashed hands to pry open the frock.

It was Majid, one of the three terrorists who'd kidnapped her and Ali and brought them to this hellhole in the Iraqi desert.

During the course of the day of captivity and travel, she'd taken measure of each of the three terrorists. Majid she had judged to be the weakest link, though he was of considerable physical bulk. He was the one who took orders while the other two were more pragmatic regarding her gender and role in this. Her kidnapping was part of something much bigger, having to do with her husband of course.

Her final assessment of Majid: a thug who did as he was told.

Still, she'd kept an eye on him during the day because of the look in his eyes. Immersed as Majid was in his world of Islamic fundamentalism, there burned a naked, sexual hunger in his gaze whenever his eyes swept over her.

But at last the day had come to an end.

Her son, Ali, had said little throughout their ordeal. The boy simply remained as close to his mother as possible, silently observing everything as they were transported from Rome where the terrorists had finally left them alone. Majid had been posted outside their door, the door closed but left unlocked.

When they were alone, Denise had spoken words of encouragement to Ali that she hoped sounded more positive than she felt. She assured Ali that his father would do everything in his power to see they were returned home safely. This would come to pass and they would be home again before long.

Ali listened, saying nothing.

She tucked him in with a mother's kiss to the forehead, and then stepped through to her connecting bedroom where she either fell asleep or simply passed out upon the bed, only to find herself awakened in the dim light of a candle with a man atop her, trying to rape her!

Reflex brought Denise instantly and completely awake, fighting to resist with an automatic strength she didn't know she had. She rolled onto her side with enough muscle behind it that her attacker was pushed off from the bed and onto the floor with a loud thud. Denise brought herself into a sitting position, becoming cognizant of her surroundings. She was alone in the room with Majid.

A belt heavy with two holsters and an assortment of knives lay cast aside on the floor. His slacks were around his ankles. The predator in him had waited until everyone was asleep.

He clumsily tried to regain his footing but before he could, Denise extended a leg, bringing her right foot around to connect with a hard blow to the side of Majid's head. The kick knocked his head against the wall. Majid fell forward onto his face.

Denise leapt from the bed to her feet. She'd enrolled in a couple of martial arts instruction courses at the gym where the Ashid family had resided, but she'd never expected to actually use concepts like using the man's weight against him as a means of self-defense.

She started for the connecting door to check on Ali.

Two things stopped her. First, her son appeared in the connecting doorway, clad in a junior male version of a frock not dissimilar to her own. The boy had obviously just been awakened by the sudden activity. And through the other door came Kemal, Majid's partner, bursting into Denise's bedroom, also drawn by the noise.

Martial arts training she'd all but forgotten flared into automatic response. Denise pivoted on one leg, delivering a wicked kick to Kemal's chest that slammed the terrorist back against the doorframe, allowing Denise the opportunity to rush in and deliver a hard kick to his balls.

Shy, sweet, innocent little Ali stood there in the connect thing doorway using both hands to rub the sleep from his eyes, staring at but not wholly comprehending the sight he was witnessing: the semi-conscious man beside the bed on hands and knees, his belt with attached pistols and knives lying there on the floor like a discarded toy. His mom taking on not one but two bad guys like some kung fu hero in a movie.

It was a reflexive response alone, nearly free of rational thought, that compelled Denise at that point to grab hold of her little boy's hand with her left hand and scoop up one of the pistols from Majid's discarded belt with the other.

She saw her chance and she was taking it. She'd kill if she had to.

She yanked Ali past the semi-conscious man, running into the narrow corridor that appeared to run the length of this single level building.

Beyond barred windows was the gloom of night. A trio of doors lined one wall of the corridor. Denise rushed to the first door.

Locked.

She hurried along the corridor, putting as much distance as she could between them and their captors. Ali kept pace, his little legs pumping to keep up without faltering. She rattled the handle of the second door but it held tight.

Locked again.

Her mind screamed at her: *No!* She and her child were not meant to die in captivity.

The third door was *not* locked.

With a gasp of relief, still hovering on the edges between sanity and panic, Denise and her boy barreled through this doorway into the crisp, cool open air of the desert night.

She cried out to her son, "Stay with me, honey! We're going to make it!"

Then came the clicking of motion detectors.

Outdoor spotlights snapped on, revealing the truth of where they were and what faced them. They had "escaped" into a barbed wire enclosed area lined with a high chain link fencing topped with barbed wire, its razor sharpness glinting in the mean light. Directly on the other side of the fencing stood a dozen Hezbollah soldiers wearing desert camo fatigues, their rifles aimed at Denise and her son. She could just make out the outline of a tank parked beyond the light.

A Syrian control officer stepped into the doorway they'd just fled through. He had introduced himself as Fared al-Hor at one point before they'd left Rome. Kemal was the one charged with their kidnapping, backed up by Majid, but it was a Fared who exuded the arrogant air of command.

Majid stood behind Fared's right shoulder, a look of apprehensive guilt seeming to weigh down his features.

Fared extended his hand, palm up.

"That will be quite enough of that, Mrs. Rashid. Majid's pistol, if you please."

Denise knew when she was beat. What a fool she'd been to think it would be so easily done; just slip away and walk off into the desert night.

She handed over the pistol to Fared and then pointed her

finger accusingly at Majid.

"You know what he was trying to do to me?"

It would hardly take much imagination. Her hair had to be a fright, her frock disheveled from the running and mishandling. But most damning of all was the guilt in Majid's eyes as he braced himself for Fared's reaction.

Fared bowed in an almost courtly fashion.

"My sincere apologies, madam. This was not meant to happen. We are professionals here. It will not happen again."

"You are professional *terrorists*," Denise snarled, knowing she was in shock, but not giving one good damn. "You kidnap and brutalize women and children. What sort of men are you?"

"Enough," snapped Fared. "Silence, woman."

He turned to Majid and swiped the side of Majid's head with his own pistol, delivering an angry rant while doing so. Majid flinched but did not block the physical assault nor the verbal one. He took his punishment, eyes downcast, shamed and humiliated. Fared finished by throwing the pistol into Majid's face. Fared stepped back with his arms crossed sternly before him. Majid scrambled to retrieve his pistol and stood there obediently awaiting further instructions.

Fared led the way back into the building. They returned along the hallway to the set of connecting rooms. Kemal had regained his strength. Fared was considering administering further punishment to Majid for his transgression. The expression Fared wore while considering such thoughts was enough to send yet more fear into Majid. Fared decided that would be enough for now.

So far the operation had gone smoothly, completely to Fared's satisfaction and to the satisfaction of his superiors in Damascus. Kemal had engineered a most audacious kidnapping in Rome earlier that very same day and here they were.

Their current spot along the Euphrates River, just inside the Iraqi-Syrian border, had once been a thriving oasis but was now as desolate and forgotten as it could be. The hot desert winds and the shifting sands take their toll on all living things. These days the "oasis" mostly consisted of overgrown weeds amid a general atmosphere of deterioration.

The presence of the Iranians in the master plan to silence Ahmed Rashid allowed Damascus to hold its distance on the world stage even if everyone did know who was behind the kidnapping and why. So far, one day in, everything was working to perfection. Fared considered the presence of the Hezbollah soldiers at this location to be vitally important. Even if the hostages were somehow tracked down and their location discovered, it remained impregnable due to the Russian-trained crack Iranian military unit. They were the best Tehran had to send. However, it seemed there must always be at least one bad apple in a barrel. In this case that was Majid.

On their return to the connected rooms, Majid was quick to regain the belt he'd earlier cast aside. He holstered his pistol, then he got down on his hands and one knee to glance about at floor level under the bed. But he did not make a production of it so it seemed a natural enough thing to do. He was frowning, uncertain about something. But he said nothing.

Fared told Denise, "I will see that one of the unit's best men will assume guard outside your door. I assure you, Mrs. Rashid, you and your son are safe here. You will not be harmed."

Mention of her son caused Denise to draw her back straight, to lift her chin, to rest a hand protectively about her son's slight shoulders.

"Don't you devils even think about coming close to my child."

Fared understood what she was talking about, saw little point in debating the issue.

Denise's son was a curious child, observing everything yet saying little even though his reality was being turned upside down in a single day; everything in his young life suddenly, violently changed. The young Ali was in some ways in awe of Fared and Kemal. Fared could see it plainly and so, of course, could the boy's mother. Ali saw their guns and their commitment conveying a kind of male power that was not part of this little boy's protective bubble of life. Seeing this, his mother was justifiably concerned about where such an unsure path could lead a child.

Fared led his men out of the two connecting rooms. Again the door was closed behind them. This time a key was turned in the lock. Somehow that made enough difference for Denise to feel a little safer.

When he was sure they were alone, Ali sat on the bed next to his mother. He pulled up the hem of his garment so Denise could see where he had hidden the knife he'd swiped from Majid's belt. Denise smiled her surprise and a trace of pride touched her heart. She indicated Ali to keep the knife hidden.

It would be their little secret.

She tucked her son into bed for the second time that night, and for once he didn't even seem to mind the mother's kiss to his forehead before she rose and left his room.

But Denise Rashid could not fall asleep that night. She could only lie awake, staring at the ceiling, listening to the vague sounds of the Hezbollah guard detail outside the house. She was worried and fearful. This was hell on earth; what she and Ali were going through, and tomorrow would bring more of the same, likely worse than today in ways she could not imagine.

How would it end?

CHAPTER SEVEN

Al Udeid Air Base, Qatar—Four hours earlier...

Naturally enough when a man has legitimately earned the nickname "Suicide," his reputation will nearly always precede him. Such was the case when Suicide Cody and Sara Durell were shown into the office of Lieutenant-Colonel Wil Stratton.

Stratton had become a highly placed command level bureaucrat who missed his days as a fighter pilot that dated back to Desert Storm. But he had not been off the front lines for so long that he couldn't sense at once the warrior spirit in a man the moment they met. That was definitely the case when Cody and the woman were shown in.

Stratton's offices were on the third floor of the Air Operations Center HQ. Two of his office walls were floor-to-ceiling plate glass windows that provided an impressive, widescreen view of the busy, sprawling airfield. The constant rumble of fighter and cargo planes landing and taking off was not intrusive but rather a natural background accent.

The minuscule nation of Qatar occupies the small Qatar Peninsula on the northeastern coast of the Arabian Peninsula, sharing its sole land border with neighboring Saudi Arabia to the south. The rest of its territory is surrounded by the Persian Gulf. An Islamic country—total population: 2.6 million—Qatar has a high-income economy backed by the world's third largest natural gas and oil reserves. Qatar has emerged as a middle power in the Arab world through its resource-wealth as well as its globally expanding media group, the Al Jazeera network.

Bilateral relations are strong with the US and Qatar coordinating closely on a wide range of regional and global issues; it's a defense partnership that provides for the security and stability of a troubled region. Qatar hosts close to 10,000 US service personnel, most of them stationed at Al Udeid. The airbase serves as logistics, command, and basing hubs for the US Central Command area of operations.

All of this made Lieutenant-Colonel Stratton's life a busy one indeed. Overseeing US air operations in Iraq, Afghanistan and Syria left little room in his world for idle chit-chat or gossip in the ranks.

But yeah, sure, he knew Suicide Cody's story, a damn sad, tragic story if ever there was one. As a CIA field operative specializing in deep cover missions, Cody had been the best. For three administrations he was The President's Man. They wrote novels and made action movies about guys like Jack Cody. He was the real deal. He took on the toughest missions around the world and always managed to pull a rabbit out of the hat and make it home safe and sound.

That is until tragedy struck.

A band of terrorists, seeking vengeance, had planted a bomb in Cody's family car. The bomb, meant to kill Cody, instead horrifically ended the lives of Cody's wife and their two small children. It was a tragedy that would knock over any man. Beneath Cody's heroic exterior beat the heart and soul of a man of normal emotions and feelings whose private world was unexpectedly and utterly blown apart, shattered and gone forever.

Cody settled that blood debt, tracking down each person responsible for what happened to his family. He'd cleared the slate and ended that cell of terrorists. And with that it should have been over. But instead Cody went underground. He stayed out of touch for more than a year and when he resurfaced, the president and former friends and associates were gladdened to see that his skillset had in no way deteriorated.

But on the inside, where everything counts, the poor guy was still tortured by grief and regret to such a degree that he wanted to end his life. Everyone knows the phrase "suicide by cop." Upon his return, what Cody offered his superiors was a variation on that: he would only accept missions that were so dangerous they held no chance of survival.

That's where the nickname "Suicide" came from.

The irony, lost on few, was that after nine such missions (or "suicide attempts"), the guy was still taking names and kicking ass. Cody had survived every one of those missions. Instead of literally killing himself with his own work, he'd only improved his skillset and his odds for survival.

Along the way, and for sure an important part of his recovery, was his relationship with Sara Durell, herself the niece of a famed CIA agent of decades earlier, who thought of herself as carrying on a family tradition. Sara had devoted her life to government service. She had been best friends with Cody and his wife before the tragic bombing occurred and it would appear that Sara's friendship with Cody had supported his mental and spiritual return.

In Stratton's mind, whatever had grown and transpired between Cody and Sara was nobody else's damn business.

And here they were in his office.

Cody, a well-proportioned man, a shade over six-feet, with eyes that could see clear to the horizon or just as clearly into your soul, missing nothing. His bearing, military. His presence, impressive.

The woman at his side? Magazine photo model if she'd wanted to be. Sara Durell carried herself with a composed presence that matched Cody's.

What a man, thought Stratton. *What a woman.* Up close you could see that there was not a trace of fatigue in their eyes or manner. That in itself was as impressive as everything else given what he knew about the mission they'd just completed in Afghanistan.

They shook hands.

"Welcome to Qatar."

Cody's grip was straightforward, all business like the man himself.

"We're only here long enough to change planes and get this

briefing," he said.

Stratton chuckled. "Likely the best way to appreciate Qatar. The world got a good look at what a harsh, oppressive dump this is during the World Cup soccer matches last year. Anyway, it's good to meet you both."

Cody and Sara each took a chair that faced Stratton's desk.

Cody said, "Let's start with the hostages. Have we pinned down their exact whereabouts?"

"Not yet," said Stratton. "That's being developed on the ground in country. As usual there are informants and the Free Syrian Army is tapping into that network with everything they've got. It's the final piece of the puzzle. The FSA is confident they're onto something real. Since that's all we've got, it's what we're running with. I'll have you inside Syria by sundown. Your destination once in country is a US Army detachment stationed in the region we're talking about. From that point the two of you will be adapting and improvising like hell."

Sara said, "Just like in Afghanistan."

"You mean with every square foot of the place being a death trap?" Stratton nodded. "Yep, just like that."

"The difference," said Cody, "being the number of players who have inserted themselves into this war."

He and Sara had obviously reviewed the current situation in Syria before touching down at Al Udeid. Stratton had expected no less but it was a relief just the same.

When violence between the strong-arm government and pro-democracy protesters first broke out more than a decade ago, hundreds of rebel factions had emerged and eventually coalesced. The stated purpose of the Free Syrian Army militias, comprised of defectors from the government armed forces, was the ousting of the ruling regime. The FSA was supplied by the CIA with aid and intelligence.

"It's wilder than the Wild West ever was," Stratton told them. "These days much of the hot fighting has cooled down. Oh, the government will still shell hospitals and bakeries with random airstrikes designed to terrorize the population and weaken rebel support but the war itself has descended into one hell of a complex battlefield. The region's geo-political rivalries are dug in and squaring away."

"Russia and Iran," said Sara. "That's a real bad mix."

"Sure is," said Stratton. "That web of competing interests is a major complication. Russia is a staunch ally. Damascus relies on Russia to conduct air strikes targeting rebel groups and to supply its army with training and the latest weaponry. As for Iran, they've offered unwavering support. Syria is one of Iran's few allies in the region. Their mutual fear and loathing of the US and Israel sustain their alliance."

"Meanwhile," growled Cody, "there's ISIS."

The Islamic State. Their aim: to return the whole damn world to the early days of pure Islam; jihadists who adhered to an extreme interpretation of the Koran. They held that the rest of the world was made up of non-believers, justifying attacks against other Muslims and non-Muslims alike. ISIS continued to claim responsibility for carrying out attacks on the US and other Western nations, posing a serious threat; a key force arrayed against the regime *and* the US.

Stratton said, "ISIS attacks are on the rise out in Deir ez-Zour Province. That's where you'll be. The province is oil rich. US troops have been deployed to protect US interests and strategic land routes and to maintain pressure on ISIS. We continue to support the FSA but our primary focus has largely shifted to counter-terrorism. Your destination is a small detachment of Delta Force soldiers and Rangers guarding a gas plant that's owned by a major American corporation. And that's about it for the cast of players you'll be dealing with. You'll have your hands full, no damn doubt about that." Stratton paused to clear his throat, then he added, "On a personal note, give 'em hell for this old combat pilot, okay?"

Sara broke the official ice with a good natured chuckle.

"You don't much care for this desk job, do you, sir?"

"The work I do here is important," said Stratton, "but you're right about that, Ms. Durell. You sure are."

"I know the feeling," said Sara. "I went through hell to break away from my desk at the Pentagon so I could get back in the field where I belong."

Cody tugged absently at an earlobe, exhibiting little patience with small talk.

He said, "Then I guess we'd better get on our way," and he started to rise.

This was the moment Stratton had *not* been looking forward to and not just because an interesting encounter with two extraordinary people was about to come to an end. He'd consciously saved for last what he had for them: the worst piece of news for Cody and Durell.

He'd enjoyed this brief encounter with these two. He liked them on a personal level, which meant he did not look forward to delivering the final piece of vital information that would more than likely make this, Cody's mission into Syria, a true suicide mission.

For the past week, military officers and intelligence analysts in Al Udeid's counter-intelligence section, seated at their computer screens, had been monitoring drone feeds of an escalating crisis inside Syria that could be on the brink of blowing the world apart.

Stratton took a deep breath, exhaled it in a rush and said, "Uh, there is one last thing..."

CHAPTER EIGHT

Camp David, Maryland

Sunshine, drenching the rolling hills, made the bark of the birch trees seem whiter and dappled through their bare branches over a winding gravel path.

Halfway into his three-mile run through the Camp David forest, the President of the United States noted with satisfaction that he was not short of breath cresting a steep rise. He'd been a confirmed two-pack-a day-man before the last election, when his campaign advisors had convinced him that a non-smoking image would be far more appealing to voters.

At 65, President Martin Harwood was a vigorous man, appearing at least a decade younger. At 5-foot-10, he weighed in at a solidly built 180 pounds. His face was naturally round, but with strong features and striking eyes. The salt and pepper hair was worn military style, unfashionably short. The fact that he was an ex-military officer, not a professional establishment politician, had contributed largely to his being selected as his party's vice presidential candidate. He was not considered attractive or elegant but exuded a straightforward style and grace that the public and the media had taken to.

He'd made some prompt and drastic changes among his predecessor's staff and cabinet, appointing a close circle of advisors who were not yes people or inside the Beltway pros, but seasoned movers and shakers in their own right. He had a well-earned reputation for toughness and fairness, for principled leadership and bipartisanship. This did not mean that everything went smoothly all of the time. There were far too many conflicting forces at work in an ever-shrinking world and a nation of 250 million for that ever to be the case.

The president concentrated on the regular rhythm of his breathing, trying to make it the primary focus of his awareness.

Secret Service agents—two on point, two to the rear and another pair traveling parallel to the jogging path on either side—maintained their position. They weren't breathing hard either. But then, they were 20 years younger than he was, he reminded himself wryly. A pair of golf carts followed, carrying more Secret Service men and a warrant officer. The WO, with a plain black briefcase chained to his wrist, was one of those specially selected custodians of the nuclear codes.

The president had called this unscheduled break in his day to recharge himself, to clear his mind. But it wasn't doing much good. It had been a day spent honing his verbal sparring skills against a hard-nosed, well-primed debater in preparation for what was supposed to be a routine press conference previously scheduled for the following day. At such press conferences, there were invariably tough, combative, sometimes unexpected soundbite questions on complex issues. The sparring partner's job was to be even tougher on him, if possible, than the traditionally bloodthirsty White House media corps would be. It had been a grueling session.

The day after the press conference, he would be attending the next European summit. His information package on the summit was 300 pages, and he hadn't cracked it yet. There remained plenty of fences there in need of mending. Business per usual in other words but, as usual, too damn much of it. He was currently hanging fire at about an even 50% approval rating in the polls. The economy continued to take three steps back for every one forward. America's involvement in the Mideast had only deepened and expanded, but there was still no light at the end of that tunnel. The Cold War was over, but its chilled dryness had made the world into a tinderbox, ready to ignite anywhere at any time. Terrorism was on the rise again, and the man who could top a hill without losing his breath remained unable to do much of anything about any of it.

Damn frustrating, yeah.

A weekend at Camp David had seemed just the thing.

The agent on point, a young man of Japanese descent, the shift leader of the detail, heard something in the miniature earpiece receiver of his shortwave radio that prompted him to give a hand signal for the run to stop. The other agents tightened in, which was their position when a golf cart bearing Jim Corbett, Harwood's Chief of Staff, rounded a bend up ahead and came to a stop.

Corbett was middle-aged, with a thinning sandy haired comb over. He was bespectacled and looked like a college professor because that's exactly what he had been before being drafted into Harwood's administration.

He said, "Sorry to interrupt you, Mr. President, but we just got word from Al Udeid."

Harwood used a forearm to wipe away the sheen of perspiration from his forehead.

He said, "Cody and Sara?"

"Stratton reports they've been processed through. Rough passage along the way but they're in."

"Thank God they made it."

"Sir, the crisis is escalating. That force we've had under observation remains unidentified. They are now halted less than a mile from the processing plant they've been approaching."

"The plant where Cody and Sara are bound?"

"Yes, sir. They should be touching down there any time now."

"And they know what's waiting for them?"

"Yes, sir. Stratton said when he told them, Cody and Durell just took it in stride."

The president chuckled.

"They would. The original dynamic duo. At least they know what lies ahead. Wish we could say the same."

"Our communication initiatives are progressing."

"Progressing but not producing," said Harwood. "We're talking about a military force of more than 500 troops, 27 vehicles including tanks and armored personnel carriers. And we don't know who they are? We don't know what such a heavily weaponized outfit is up to, advancing on us like they are. We only know they're talking Russian to each other across their damn TAC net. Not only that but they start marching toward on an oil company facility owned by an American corporation that's under our protection. What the hell, Jim? What can we do that we haven't done? We need answers."

"We're leaning on the Russian command in Syria but they're stonewalling every step of the way," said Corbett. "They assure us the force is not theirs—repeat, *not theirs*—and so they claim to have no control over it. But it's clear-cut. The Russians stay on their side of the Euphrates, we stay on our side and we continue separate offensives against ISIS. But without notification or warning this "unknown" outfit assembles near the river and crosses from the Russian controlled zone onto our side. The Pentagon is demanding an explanation from the Kremlin"

"Shit," said the president.

"More stonewalling. That relationship was cool before this mess broke."

"A time of high geopolitical tension," said Harwood, "and now this. The military forces of one nuclear superpower directly facing off against hundreds of heavily armed and hostile citizens of another nuclear superpower, who may or may not be acting at the behest of that superpower. Okay. If they want to operate outside the parameters of diplomacy that, given the circumstances, doesn't leave us much of a choice."

Corbett nodded his understanding.

He said, "Cody. But he's on another mission, sir. The Rashid kidnapping. Do we contact him?"

"Not yet," said the president thoughtfully. "This is going to be a tough one. It's going to be a long night and I'd like to see us all in one piece come morning. Let's see what Cody does next."

CHAPTER NINE

The landing zone was a barren four acres that comprised the small, dusty military outpost adjacent to the natural gas plant. The piping, storage tanks and equipment of the plant were brightly lit but there was no one in sight.

As for the army base, there were no trees. There was no color under the night lights except for the coating of dusty sand that blanketed everything: bunkers, vehicles and personnel. Machine gun emplacements were at intervals along the perimeter. Artillery and mortars were inside the compound.

This all vanished behind a veil of dust, a sand storm kicked up by the chopper's backwash as Aboo gently touched down the helicopter. He initiated a systems slowdown. The little chopper's engine noise and rotor RPMs went into idle mode.

Cody gave the young pilot a grateful pat on the shoulder, then he wasted no time exiting the helicopter and striding toward a welcoming committee of two soldiers who stood waiting nearby.

The night air had cooled considerably since their arrival in the country such a short while ago. Out here in the barren wasteland of this remote desert, the sand and rocks quickly lost their heat once the sun has disappeared behind the horizon. The temperature was in the mid-fifties.

Sara paused beside the helicopter. She turned to Aboo who remained seated at the controls. There had been little to no opportunity for conversation during the flight from Damascus due to the loud, steady rumble of the helo's flight noise combined with the fact that the privately owned little aircraft came equipped with only one set of headphones, thus making communication between the three extremely difficult.

Aboo had performed his piloting duties like a seasoned pro, keeping their flight lights off and, to avoid detection by radar, staying so close to the moonlit terrain speeding by beneath that it felt close enough to reach out and touch. They skirted what Sara determined to be the As-Suwayda hill region, an inhospitable area of wind-swept rock stony slopes and cliffs. While piloting them here from Damascus, Aboo was surely in the depths of mournful torment ever since Sara had felt compelled to share the news before takeoff of Aisha Hassan's death. He sat there now, intently making a last-minute check of gauges and dials on the dashboard before him.

She said, "Aboo," speaking only loud enough to catch his attention through the diminished rumble of the helicopter's idling.

He looked up absently, meeting her gaze as if having forgotten she existed, so distracted was he by his grief. It was difficult in this light to read his eyes.

Aboo said, before she could speak further, "I cannot wait. I must be gone. I must return to Damascus; to Aisha."

Sara heard that as a statement with two interpretations: one was that there would be much to be done in the aftermath of the girl's death. Arrangements, cover-ups, dealing with the family, etc. And yet Sara had seen cases of battlefield traumatic shock. Aboo's words could also indicate that, even given the time spent making the flight here, the poor guy had not yet accepted his sweetheart's fate. Did he expect to see her again?

Sara said, "You've done great service, getting us this far. But you're under too much stress right now to make the flight back. You saw those troops amassed as we came in just now. There's trouble coming, and you'll be much safer here on a US military base than up there alone flying through the night." He sat there listening to her but he offered no response and so she added, "Think about it, Aboo. Please, as a favor to me."

He said, "I have no more time. I am needed in Damascus. Goodbye, American lady. May Allah guide and protect you."

"And you," were Sara's parting words to him.

She stepped away from under the 'copter's overhead blades as Aboo increased their RPM's by initiating the pre-takeoff procedure. Sara turned to make her way to where Cody was already engaged in conversation with the two soldiers.

Sara clearly sensed the air of heightening anticipation like an electrical current. The night was alive with shouted orders and coarse energy, exhaust fumes and the clicking and clanking of engines, equipment and weaponry being prepped and positioned. Nearly every soldier in sight was toting a rifle and a wary attitude.

When he saw her approaching, Cody interrupted his conversation with the two soldiers.

"Sara Durell, this is Captain Larson, Executive Officer in charge here."

"Captain," said Sara with a nod.

The CO looked to be around thirty. Medium of build, regulation-short red hair, a sprinkling of freckles across pale features unlined by age, experience or contemplative thought. The guy was tensed up like everybody else here tonight. But instead of determination, Sara read uncertainty and fear in his eyes and manner. A pair of night vision binoculars hung around his neck.

Larson said with the hint of a sneer in his voice, "I'll tell you what I just told Cody here. I'd say welcome, but if you're at all sane, you'd rather be someplace else."

The soldier standing next to Larson was a strapping man somewhere in his late 40s with a coffee latte complexion and E-6 stripes on his sleeve.

He interjected with a chuckle, "Hell, sir, that goes for every one of the 40 boys here tonight." He added, with an engaging toothy smile that cut through a battle-toughened demeanor, "Evening, ma'am."

Cody said, "Sergeant Samuels. Top kick of this detachment.

"Sergeant," said Sara, giving him a nod.

Her reading was that this incident—whatever was behind it, whatever was going to happen—was the closest an untested commanding officer had ever gotten to the fire; not so his top sergeant.

Larson started to say something but was drowned out by the noise of the helicopter lifting off. Its landing and flight lights remained off as Aboo piloted the diminutive aircraft into a smooth takeoff. The noise gradually diminished as the copter faded from sight, virtually disappearing into the night sky.

Larson resumed their conversation.

"You two have come a long way for nothing. You're pretty much screwed, if you want my opinion. Your Free Syrian Army friends haven't shown up yet. You're supposed to rendezvous with them here and go after that American lady who who's married to the sand crab, right?"

Cody said, "No one's working from a script. The FSA will come through and we'll have the Intel we need. It doesn't always happen on schedule. Name of this game is adapt and improvise."

"Is that right? Huh. You're risking your life on a dumb mission, cowboy. You, too, cowgirl. That Mrs. Rashid should've stayed with her own kind. Like everything else out here tonight, your mission is totally screwed up. Not only that but it's interfering with what we're dealing with here tonight."

Sara said, "How are we interfering?"

Larson glowered at her. He didn't have much use for uppity women. He started to respond, but then the night sky suddenly lit up like a Fourth of July fireworks from the direction taken by the helicopter, followed seconds later by the boom of the explosion, like thunder accompanying the angry, blossoming orange-red explosion that flared ever so briefly before fading in upon itself, followed by the clatter of the helicopter's burnt-out wreckage crashing to the desert floor some distance away.

Cody said, "That could only have been a SAM fired from that force you've got camped up the road."

"Camped? Whoever they are, that outfit isn't *camped*. Mister, we just witnessed their opening shot! I had two drones here but they're sacked through lack of maintenance. But we do know there's 500 of *them* and we know there's 40 of *us*. Whoever they are, they're getting ready to eat us alive."

Sergeant Samuels cleared his throat. He sent Cody and Sara a glance of discomfort before saying, "Uh, sir, that sort of talk won't help anything."

Larson stared off into the distance where the copter had gone down.

He said, "At least it wasn't one of my men or one of our choppers that went down. No casualties. Not yet, anyway."

Sara said, "We are being paid to be here, Sergeant, whether we like it or not. The young man flying that helicopter was a civilian. A volunteer. He was no soldier, just another victim of this war. Poor Aboo."

"Their war, not ours," snapped Larson. "The only reason we're here is a big-ass oil company in the states wants to keep their oil flowing. So there's a detachment of 40 men under my command facing off a mechanized, heavily armed military force of 500. Nobody knows who they are or what's happening and I've been ordered not to take any sort of proactive measure that could provoke a confrontation." Larson's voice climbed as his rant went on. "An American gunship out of here has been missing and unaccounted for with its entire crew since yesterday. And now you two show up on some world-shaking mission that's already off-track. What if your FSA friends don't show up? What if they're dead, lying out there in the desert? What then?"

Sergeant Samuels said, "Sir, you need to slow it down a notch. You're stressed out. Every man on this base is uptight about whatever's going to happen next. But like the lady said, we're soldiers. This is what we're paid to do."

Cody added, "Your top kick has it right, Captain. This will—"

"Don't anybody tell me this will work out," snarled Larson. "We'll be lucky if we don't all die tonight." He raised the binoculars from around his neck and stared off in the direction of the encampment. Then he snarled again. "Damn it to hell, I can't see a god damn thing." He jerked the binoculars from around his neck and threw them to the ground. He said, "I need a break!"

Sara, Cody and the E-6 watched him storm away.

Sara rolled her eyes.

"That's rich. The boy's in over his head. I could use a break my own self."

Cody humored her with a chiding, "Maybe after tonight."

He picked up the binoculars.

CHAPTER TEN

With the NVD binoculars, Cody scanned the terrain beyond the Army base and gas plant. At first there was nothing to see in the shimmering green light as magnified by the night vision device, only the blank wall of night meeting the featureless earthen desert floor. Then he panned in the direction from where they'd seen the sprawl of activity during landing. There was also little to see in that direction. A small collection of dilapidated mobile homes and houses loomed a half-mile away along a rough dirt road, the only sign of human habitation beyond the base.

As Cody considered what he saw through the binoculars, he became aware of Samuels watching him.

He asked the sergeant, "What am I looking at?"

"That's where the local employees of the gas plant reside. You must have noticed the plant was shut down when you folks landed."

Sara said, "I didn't see anyone working there. Looked like it was locked down."

"That's because it is closed down," said Samuels. "It's been few days now since this bunch breathing down on us were first spotted. The closer they got, the more the folks working at the plant decided it might be a good idea to be somewhere else. Kind of like our gallant commander."

Cody lowered the binoculars, handing them to Sara.

"Been meaning to talk to you about that, Top. He's not the only officer around here, is he?"

"Technically, no. There's pair of second louies in the mix but they're as wet behind the ears as Larson."

"In other words," said Cody, "you're the man running the show here."

Samuels shrugged mildly.

"Just doing my job, Mr. Cody. But yeah, I reckon the boys here do sort of look up to me. I've had a piece of the action, one way or another, in every scrape Uncle Sam has taken a part since Grenada. Remember that one? Course you do but a lot of the young 'uns don't. This here is a good bunch, you can bet on that. These are Rangers and Delta Force. But yeah, you put me on the spot so I'll cop to it. Why you want to know something like that?"

Cody said, "Durell and I are here with White House authorization. If that bunch down the road does close in tonight, we may be obligated to take command here. If that becomes the case, I need to know what and who we're dealing with."

Samuels' eyes grew thoughtful.

"Take command, eh? That is big talk, mister. The CO, he's

right about one thing. Our asses *are* on the line. We are talking 40 against 500. But you're the savior sent from on high to pull us out of this mess, is that it?"

"But only with your help," said Cody, not wishing to engage in debate with the guy. As always, time was of the essence. He said, "Get through to Lieutenant-Colonel Stratton at Al Udeid. He'll back up every word I'm telling you. So this force is on the other side of that neighborhood, using it for cover."

"It's been like this since the middle of the afternoon, them not doing a damn thing. That's when our CO started getting real squirrely. Up until then everyone was hoping it was some sort of training exercise the Ruskies have going on, just messing with us. Now, with them this close..."

Sara lowered the NVD binoculars, having had a look through them.

"It sure as hell isn't going to stay like this," she said. "Where does that leave us, Cody?"

Cody said, "There's one way to get a pedigree on that bunch that hasn't been tried yet."

Sara surveyed Cody with narrowed eyes. "Are you thinking what I think you're thinking?" she asked. "We are on a mission and that's not it."

"No one's forgetting about Denise Rashid and her son," said Cody. "We'll radio Stratton to determine if there's any new Intel on them. If there isn't, well, I'm not going to sit here waiting for something to happen."

"Uh, if you don't mind my asking, sir," said Samuels, "what are you going to do?"

Sara said, "He's going to make a soft probe. He's going to find someone who knows and he's going to ask them who they are and what they're up to."

Samuels look skeptically from one of them to the other.

"Be serious now."

"Oh, I'm serious and so is Mr. Cody. Am I right, Jack?"

"As always," said Cody with a grin. He turned to Samuels. "I'm traveling light, Sergeant. Here's what I'll need."

Samuels was staring at Cody with undisguised curiosity.

"You're honestly going over there on your own to confront them?"

"It's what he does," said Sara.

Cody said again, "Here's what I'll need."

* * * * *

Twenty minutes later, Sara stood next to Sergeant Samuels at a relatively quiet corner of the Army compound. There'd been a hurried, chaste hug exchanged with Cody. No kiss. This was work. And then he was on his way.

Cody wore all black. His cheek bones and forehead also blackened, so that he became indiscernible in the night within seconds of sprinting beyond the reach of the base lights. He literally became one with the night.

She lost sight of him.

She knew the world of men better in many respects than she knew the ways of her own gender. After all, she'd grown up with for older brothers. Mother died of cancer when Sara was only three. Her father and brothers raised her. Her father was a good man, a successful business executive. Naturally, as the baby of the family and the only girl, she was her father's spoiled little angel. This, however, only made it worse for her when it came to the general harassment and teasing of her rough-housing, free-spirited brothers. Little surprise then that she became a dyed in the wool tomboy. At an early age Sara could ride a horse or pitch baseball better than any boy her age. Her brothers taught her how to shoot.

And so, yes, having been raised by men, she knew more than a little about their nature and their ways.

Sara had achieved this while somehow retaining the mystique of her femininity, the qualities that made her a woman. She knew from experience that men found her attractive, even desirable. She'd been married once—they were both too young and that was long ago—but had spent most of her adult life living up to her personal potential; keeping herself healthy and productive. Her climb through the good old boy hierarchy of the CIA had been as arduous as it was rewarding.

Then Cody came into her life.

They had been through so much that by this time she could read the man like a book. Not that Jack Cody was an easy man to read. Had it been his nature to gamble, he would have made one hell of a poker player. He rarely revealed to the world what he felt inside except through his actions. Nerves of steel. Honest and quiet and sudden death to anyone who crossed him.

That was the man they called Suicide Cody.

This mission into Syria was hardly their first rodeo together. Sara had conditioned herself not to let concern eat at her gut at moments like this. That would only distract her. She was hardly being left behind on the sidelines.

She liked Sergeant Samuels. While Captain Lawrence was a pathetic mess, she didn't see a single soldier walking about who didn't look buff, determined and ready to breathe fire.

Between the mounting crisis tonight from a superior, unknown force outside to the matter of Captain Larson unable to lead, there would be much this night to keep her and Sergeant busy.

CHAPTER ELEVEN

Cody crouched at the corner of the first structure he reached. Overhead, the black dome of night overhead glittered with countless stars. As sounds of the Army base had faded away behind him, the desert had seemed to close in, embracing him with its utter silence. The only sound discernible as he jogged along was the whisper of a night breeze sending loose sand hissing across the desert floor.

The Glock 9mm rode at his right hip. A Ka-Bar knife was sheathed at mid-chest.

The specter that was Cody advanced across the kill zone, maintaining a zigzag course in his approach to the cluster of shabby house trailers that had been home to the gas plant workers.

Traveling the one-mile distance separating the Army base from this little community, Cody considered the fact that soldiers of the Free Syrian Army had not yet shown up at the

Army base. What did that mean? Were they intercepted and killed before they could reach the base? Of course, this was all happening in a war zone so there could be any number of reasonable explanations for their delayed arrival. A war zone is a place of constantly shifting realities. A couple hours late? Nothing to be overly concerned with at this point. And the bottom line: Cody didn't intend leave without Denise Rashid and her son.

The objective now was to identify this group encamped so close to the American base. The unidentified force was situated directly on the other side of this cluster of trailers. There wasn't much noise from there at the moment, only the idling of truck engines accompanied by the smell of exhaust fumes that came and went depending on the breeze.

Cody felt fairly certain this wasn't the official Russian military he was infiltrating. That is, they were not operating on direct orders from Moscow. That possibility must be under consideration up and down the US chain of command, thus begging the question: *who*? Who was backing this rogue military operation; all these men, the trucks and tanks? Who was running the show? Who was in command here?

There was only one way to find out.

Why conclude that the Russian government was not behind this bunch? Hell, if they were, by this time the Kremlin would have offered up something in justification, if not explanation or defense. They wouldn't be shrugging their shoulders, scratching their heads and pleading ignorance. Cody didn't think they were ignorant of any damn thing. But their posture strongly suggested their lack of direct control over whatever was happening here. It was out of their hands.

This was some sort of private military operation.

Would there ever be a time when the US wasn't tasked with busting down the bad guys who wanted to make trouble? Cody didn't think so. And right now "bad guys" were personified in the form of this outfit, so well-armed and speaking Russian, advancing on the gas plant and the small group of American soldiers protecting it.

It would likely always be that way. Since 1776, Cody's country had embodied a moral center and intent that has changed history. Once people get a taste of personal freedom, they want more, whether they live in China or Saudi Arabia or Alabama, USA. Every world power before America sustained itself through enslaving the conquered and pillaging their natural resources. Rebuilding Japan after World War II was just was one example of that moral center expressing itself. Trying to bring justice and democracy to Afghanistan was another example.

Sometimes it worked, sometimes it didn't.

America mirrored the human condition with all its potentials and, yeah, with plenty of flaws thanks to a little thing called human nature. There was plenty about America to improve on and to bitch about. You couldn't argue that. But to Cody's way of thinking, taking over the world with McDonald's and Coca-Cola franchises and democracy rather than bombs, death and the misery of war was definitely a sign of progress.

Would such progress ever be truly global? That, as Shakespeare wrote, was "a consummation devoutly to be wished for." And if such a road ahead could be envisioned, could it not then be someday traveled? Someday could seem like a long, long way off. For now, it was enough that the big difference was in America, terrorism was a crime. In Syria, it was business as usual.

At the moment, Cody's attention stayed focused on what he had to do next: negotiate the disorganized labyrinth of these dilapidated trailers. There was some lighting, though not much, from what was obviously these troops' temporary position; some of that lighting spilled over into the labyrinth, not illuminating much of it but rather creating a maze of shadow. Cody did not mind the shadows. He welcomed them. He used them, advancing with extreme caution from trailer to trailer, from shadow to shadow.

A two-man patrol came ambling along. They passed close enough for Cody to overhear the low mumble of their conversation. They were speaking Russian and, while Cody spoke some rudimentary Russian, he could not make out their exact words, only that they seemed to be commiserating, griping over having to be on their own, away from the others, sharing the universal soldier's lot that is sentry duty. Neither of the sentries gazed anywhere near his position in the shadows. They ambled on their way, wholly unaware of the infiltrator's presence.

Cody had a plan for gaining the information here that he

needed, a plan included not raising any sort of disturbance that would call attention and reveal his presence before he even got inside their perimeter. He'd prefer not having to kill on the way in or at all for that matter. This was a "soft probe," its intention being to gain information, not inflict damage.

* * * * *

After having served three weeks in Syria, Dimitri Volkov had come to the conclusion that being a mercenary was the worst line of work a fellow could find. At 39-years-old, Dimitri had already lived several lives: There was a wife and two daughters somewhere in the world that he'd lost track of long ago; He'd been a criminal, working a dozen low-level, semi-legal and illegal enterprises, or scams, that unfortunately had not been quite low level enough to escape the attention of harsh authorities, drawing Dimitri a sentence of 20 years' hard labor. He'd considered that to be a life sentence given his inability to buckle under and the sheer brutality of life in a Russian prison.

Then came his life as a mercenary.

They'd recruited him from where he was serving his sentence at an east Moscow prison. He and 200 other convicts listened to "a guest speaker" imported by the prison officials. The man was a rugged-looking Russian with a military bearing. He referred to himself as a spokesperson for an organization he only referred to as The Group.

"Only God can get you out of this prison," he told them, "and that will be in a coffin. But I can get you out today. If you sign up, we will feed you, train you and put you on the front lines. If you retreat or disobey an order, we'll shoot you, no questions asked. If you're still alive at the end of six months, you're free." He concluded with the claim that across Russia, 20,000 convicts had already signed up and were serving the Group.

Dimitri signed up with enthusiasm.

He and the hard-bitten man he'd signed up with were taken to a walled training facility somewhere in the countryside. They were kept under armed guard. First came a month-long, grueling physical regimen designed to physically prepare them for combat. By the second month of training, they'd become trusted enough to begin a strenuous two weeks of combat training. During that phase his weekly pay started as direct deposits into an account set up for him by The Group.

Dimitri and several hundred other Group soldiers, eager to earn their pay, had then been sent to Africa to do dirty work for a military junta in Mali, targeting civilian leaders for execution. Massacres were an effective way of eroding rebel support. Dimitri's front line duties had included torture and the destruction of the civilian infrastructure. Rape was considered a side benefit. Women encountered during the fighting often had no one or any means of protecting themselves with so many of their men dead or away fighting. After Africa came the Ukraine. Months of fierce fighting around Izium in the Kharkov region.

With winter coming on, it was a relief to find his next assignment to be in the warm—make that hot!—climate of Syria. By the time this mission was wrapped up, Dimitri's contracted six months of serving time in The Group would be at an end. Dimitri had no intention of re-enlisting. He'd done what he'd signed on to do. He'd killed people. He'd done terrible things. Unlike many who'd gone in with him, he'd managed to survive, all so he could regain personal freedom in society. Now he had enough money in his account to break away from this life of bloodshed and constant personal danger.

So far, for the past six weeks, this Syrian job had been no big deal. The organized process involved in getting all these men and equipment into place exhibited The Group's thoroughness and finesse. But, as usual, the rank and file like Dimitri was being kept totally in the dark.

The military maneuvers—their outfit crossing the Euphrates, establishing this night camp within a mile of the gas plant and US Army detachment—had gone off without a problem. The shooting down of the helicopter leaving the base could have might well have initiated a response. Dimitri had half expected the Americans to open fire. But they had held their fire.

What was it all about? Dimitri and every other mercenary in this unit were obeying orders. Not asking questions. Ready to fight and kill. Awaiting only further orders. That's the way it had gone down in Africa and in the Ukraine. Why should Syria be any different?

Dimitri wished he had not been assigned to walk his sentry beat alone. With the anticipation of upcoming action whispering through the ranks, with the troop carrier trucks and tanks idling and the mercs lounging, checking their weapons, ready for whatever command came down, that would certainly be preferable to this lonely post by himself with nothing but his thoughts to keep him company.

Would they be taking on the US Army unit defending the gas plant? He would give an honest accounting of himself tonight and after this was over, his six months with The Group would be over and done with and he could return to civilian life a free man with money in his pocket.

Dimitri decided to take a piss. He slung his rifle over his shoulder and stepped into the deepest shadows he could find, away from the idling trucks and the moonlight. He did his business. He had just finished buttoning himself up when he sensed a strange shift in these shadows.

A muscular forearm like steel locked into position under his throat, jerking his head back so his body was plastered against the man who had come up behind him. Something cold, so cold it could only be the blade of a knife, came to rest against his jugular vein, extended due to the angle at which his head was cocked.

A voice whispered in Russian in his ear. "Do you want to live or die?"

"No one wants to die," said Dimitris.

He was gasping for breath. At his response, the forearm hold relaxed ever so slightly, allowing Dimitri to regain his breath.

The voice said, "Do you speak English?"

"Yes."

"Are you Russian military?"

"No. Are you going to kill me?"

"That depends on you. You're private military. Who for?"

"RTL."

Cody had never heard of the RTL. Such private military firms had become a key component of counterinsurgency warfare, carrying out dirty deeds where the client government doesn't want to reveal its hand.

"Who's in command here?"

"General Pornov."

"Where is he?"

Regaining his breath did nothing to relax Dimitri. He sensed how close he was to dying. The touch of the blade against his jugular made the blood run cold as ice through his veins. Dimitri had no intention of dying at this man's hand if there was any chance of living. He had not come this far to die before cashing in on all the risk and effort of the past six months.

He said, "I can show you where the general is."

"Show me," said the intruder.

With the knife's icy blade remaining against his jugular and the forearm of steel holding him in place, Dimitri made ungainly progress step by step, the man allowing Dimitri the freedom to move in the direction he chose.

The trailers around them were all dark. When they reached a corner of the next trailer, the panorama of personnel, trucks and equipment opened up for them from where they stood in the shadows. As best he could in the standing headlock the man had him in, Dimitri pointed.

"There."

Along this row of structures, an occasional house interspersed the trailers. The houses were in the same condition as the trailers, ramshackle and deserted.

Except for one.

Light glimmered from the rear of a modest little, low-roofed structure, more of a shed than a house, about twenty yards from where Dimitri and Cody stood. They were staring at its backside while the front of the house faced the assembled group of men and equipment.

As he moved from shadows of the trailer to gain the shadows behind the house, Cody glimpsed that sprawling scene. He registered the same vibe of restless anticipation in the atmosphere here as he'd left behind at the Army base; the vibe of a lit, burning fuse that has just about reached the stick of dynamite.

This night was about to blow wide open and everyone on both sides knew it.

The intruder's hold on Dimitri relaxed, the forearm removed from across his throat, the frigid touch of the blade listed his jugular.

Cody said, "I'm going to pop you one and leave you here. You won't be out long. There's going to be some unscheduled excitement around here in few minutes. Understand?"

"Yes." Dimitri's breathing was shallow. Relief coursed through him. "Yes," he repeated. "I understand."

Cody said, "This conversation. You confronted me and I put you down for your trouble."

"Thank you, whoever you are."

"I'd say go in peace," said Cody, "but I don't believe that's going to be possible tonight."

He clipped the sentry behind the ear using the fist holding

the knife so that the handle impacted the right spot. Cody sheathed the knife mid-chest in time to catch the collapsing, unconscious sentry's figure.

He could have taken time to interrogate the man further but his intention was to go straight to the top. The sentry wouldn't know the big picture anyway. An act of aggression was imminent. The perpetrators had been identified.

But *why?*

That's what Washington would want to know.

It's what Cody intended to find out.

He heard footfalls approaching. He held his position, his back against the trailer, standing over the unconscious form at his feet. He unleathered the Glock 9mm, his finger curling around the trigger.

A two-man sentry patrol passed close by. Same two guys as before, still yammering about whatever it was they were yammering about. They rounded a corner and were gone.

Cody waited several more heartbeats to assure himself that there was no one else nearby. Then he left those deep shadows, making his way toward the little house with the lighted window.

CHAPTER TWELVE

They were loaded for bear.

Cody was again one with the night, gliding almost invisibly from the nearest trailer toward the back of the structure from which a lighted window glowed. Some of the illumination from out front spilled back here but not much. The throaty rumble of idling truck engines, along with the palpable vibe of anticipation, was in the air. Darting to the rear of the house, he was able, in those fleeting seconds, to assess the outfit gathered behind the row of trailers and houses.

Heavy duty shit!

Twenty or more vehicles were lined up with engines running and headlights on. Most of the trucks were armored personnel carriers surrounded by loitering mercenaries armed with assault rifles. They were accompanied by three Russian-made T-72 tanks, vehicles weighing nearly 50 tons and armed with 125 mm guns.

Cody approached the rear of the house, pressing his back

flat against its rear wall, close to the back door. The Glock up and ready, he inched closer toward the small window next to the door. He could hear voices from inside speaking in heavily accented English. From his position he could not yet clearly discern what they were saying. It was common these days around the world, in places where a language barrier interfered with communication, that the conversation switched to English, the universal language.

When he reached the window next to the door, Cody cautiously placed an eye to its low corner, hoping like hell that the black cosmetic goo applied to his cheekbones and forehead would, against the blackness of night, make him invisible to anyone inside.

Those inside were too involved in their conversation to be looking out windows. The room was barren except for the field table which held a lamp, tablet and cell phone. The window was open, allowing Cody to overhear the conversation.

A Syrian guy in civilian clothes was speaking. He wore glasses, had a mustache and slicked back hair.

"And so in conclusion, General, I would only pass along from Damascus our government's best wishes for tonight and commend you and the RTL Group for the fine job you are doing."

Cody thought, *Ah ha.*

The second man was a husky, crewcut Russian in the desert cammies. A holstered pistol rode high on his hip. Pornov.

"Tonight will be a night of victory for the Group and for Syria, friend Mahmoud," said the General. "We have already brought down a helicopter and they have yet to respond. The Americans cower. They fear what will happen if they attack us. The night belongs to us. The moment of truth is at hand. And may I make a suggestion, my friend? You had best find yourself adequate cover. Stay behind here when we advance. As the Americans would say, all hell is about to break loose."

They both chuckled at that.

Mahmoud said, "Quite right, General. Good luck to you."

"With the sort of firepower I have at my command tonight," said Pornov, "luck will hardly be necessary."

With that, the Syrian let himself out.

This left Pornov alone. But who knew how long that would last? Something big was going down tonight obviously. At any moment the front door could open and the General would be joined by one or more subordinates.

It was now or never.

When Cody came in through the rear door, Pornov's back was to him. The Russian was reaching for the computer tablet on the field desk. Cody made no effort at stealth and the general heard him and swung about, reaching for his pistol.

Cody straight-arm aimed the Glock, drawing a bead on the spot between Pornov's eyes.

In English Cody said, "Don't even think about it."

The General stayed his hand from the holstered pistol. "Who the devil are you? How did you get in here?"

As Cody expected, Pornov spoke English.

Cody said, "Unholster the piece using two fingers. Kick it over here."

Pornov understood but it took him a moment to process the request. The keen eyes of a razor sharp mind were gauging the odds. Pornov's eyes never left Cody's. He removed his pistol from its holster with the utmost care as instructed. The handgun skittered across the wooden floor from a mild kick.

Cody left the piece where it rested in a corner. Every second counted now. He'd already sized up this situation...except for the damned *why*.

Pornov said, "Now we talk, eh?"

The guy was tough as nails and cold as ice, hardly behaving the way an ordinary man would when facing a Glock 9mm aimed directly between his eyes. General Pornov was damn sure of himself. A formidable adversary.

Cody said, "What's the RTL Group doing here?"

"Ah, you know who we are."

"Talk. Waste my time and I'll kill you."

Pornov registered a small, smug smile. "Not with a handgun, surely. That would draw attention. I guarantee you would not leave here alive no matter my fate."

Cody said, "Don't be too sure of yourself, fella. I want information. Mahmoud's presence says a lot. The RTL Group is working for the Syrians. Not much of a mystery there. Okay, I've got that. Now I'm after motive."

"You do appreciate," said Pornov as if agreeably explaining something to a friend, "no matter what happens to me, no matter what you do, you will not leave here alive. You're a dead man walking...fella," he added, a chiding glint in his icy gaze.

"Talk," said Cody along his extended arm and the barrel of

the Glock.

It was a command.

Pornov registered a mild shrug. "Very well. You will not live to repeat it. Our financial chain with Syria is rather complex. Suffice to say we have contracted with the Syrian energy ministry to receive a 25% share of oil and gas produced over the next five years in any Syrian fields. Processing plants and infrastructure that RTL helps to liberate, protect and develop."

It didn't take Cody more than a heartbeat to process that one. He said, "So your Group has essentially been tasked with seizing and protecting oil and gas fields from the rightful owners on behalf of the Syrian government."

"Precisely," said Pornov with a satisfied nod.

Then he went into action.

With a lightning speed that nearly defied belief, the General's right foot rose in a martial arts kick that sent the Glock sailing from Cody's numbed fingers. Pornov made a gesture with his palms placed together, touching them to his forehead. He breathed deeply through his nose and out his mouth.

Great, thought Cody. *The guy's into kung fu. This will be a fight to the death.* He assumed a "horse stance," feet shoulder width apart, body sideways to present a narrow target.

Pornov suddenly flashed his hands in twin arches and snapped a kick for Cody's groin. Cody blocked the attack with a palm stroke to his opponent's ankle, sending a stab of pain shooting along Cody's arm. He welcomed the pain. The kick that had knocked the Glock from his hand had not injured him, merely numbed his hand for an instant. The jolt of pain along his arm let him know that feeling had returned.

His hand rose and backhanded Pornov's right arm, sweeping it aside to expose the man's right side to attack. Cody thrust the stiffened fingers of his other hand into the cluster of nerves under Pornov's right arm. The Russian cried out and staggered backward. His right arm trembled as he clasped his left hand to his pain-laced armpit. Cody whirled sharply and thrust a hard rear kick to his opponent's abdomen.

Pornov folded with a groan.

This was Cody's chance to finish off the guy and get the hell out of here. He slashed a "foot sword" to Pornov's face, the edge of his boot smashing into the general's cheekbone. Pornov fell to the floor, rolled and came to his hands and knees. He shouted out a primal war cry and lunged forward. He tried a short kick, a feint, followed by a high kick aimed at Cody's face.

Cody hustled backward, avoiding the flashing feet of his opponent. Pornov thrust a ram's head punch for Cody's solar plexus. A praying mantis block parried the punch and pulled Pornov off balance. Cody slashed the side of his hand to Pornov's neck and kicked him in the chest, his heel striking sternum bone forcibly.

Pornov tumbled again but this time landed close to his pistol on the floor. He grabbed at it and started to track the weapon around on Cody. This time it was Cody who executed a snap-kick that knocked the gun out of Pornov's hand. Pornov hauled himself to his feet. Several bruises and welts had split open. Blood oozed from his face as he started forward. Crimson drool bubbled from his lips. He was in bad shape, barely able to remain upright, yet the Russian made one last desperate effort. He lunged at Cody and swung both fists at Cody's torso.

Cody's hands struck like twin axe blades. He chopped Pornov's arms aside and instantly struck out with a two-finger thrust aimed at Pornov's face as the Russian was coming at him. Pornov grunted in pain. He stumbled back as blood poured from his eye sockets. Cody poised his hand in a spear hand fashion and launched his final stroke. The tips of his fingers struck Pornov's solar plexus. His hand stabbed, driving terrific force into Pornov's chest cavity.

The Russian's heart ruptured. General Pornov was dead on his feet. He collapsed to the floor, dead as they come.

At that precise moment, as if on a cosmic cue from the universe, the front door opened and Mahmoud came waltzing in.

The Syrian was about to say something—maybe an afterthought from his conversation with Pornov or maybe with some news from Damascus—but one look at the scene before him and the guy's eyes popped wide behind his glasses. His jaw dropped. He spun around in the doorway and started out.

Cody unsheathed the Ka-Bar and flung it fast enough to stop Mahmoud before he could get out. The knife sank to the hilt between the Syrian's shoulder blades. Then Cody was on his feet, rushing across the small room to reach Mahmoud before the fellow made it outside. Cody gripped the walking dead guy before Mahmoud could pitch forward out of the doorway, into the bright lights and personnel of the mobilizing force out front of the house. He pulled Mahmoud back in with one strong swing of his arm while closing the door with his other hand.

Cody retrieved his knife. He retrieved the Glock that had been kicked from his hand. He pocketed Pornov's cell phone and slipped the computer under his shirt. He bee-lined for the back door. He flung the door aside and dashed out into the night.

That's when his luck ran out.

A two-man sentry patrol was just coming around a rear corner of the little house. Same two guys as before, still gabbing to each other about whatever. This time there was no seeking out shadows for cover. This time it was face to face. Their eyes widened with a surprised reaction upon sighting the black-clad intruder who seemed to be half man and half night. They scrambled to track their rifles around on him.

Cody's first target was the one on the right. A 9mm slug from the Glock took off a third of the guy's head, splashing his partner with blood, brains and skull fragments. This did not deter the second guy from tracking his rifle into target acquisition. Cody went into a forward dive just as that sentry blasted a round that sizzled through space where Cody had stood seconds earlier. Cody hit the ground, his left hand softening the impact of his chest hitting the ground while he triggered off two more rounds before the sentry could lower his aim. These rounds caught the second sentry in the chest, dropping his dead body across the first.

The group that was massed out front of the house came to new life.

Even with the thunder of gunfire receding in his ears, Cody could hear the immediate reaction of shouts and commands.

There would already be men hurrying to investigate. He snagged a rifle off one of the dead sentries and fired a half clip on full auto at nothing in particular.

That prompted hesitation on the part of the advancing mercs, providing enough delay for him to move. By the time the bodies were found, the man who was one with the night was gone.

CHAPTER THIRTEEN

Summers, the CIA control officer in Rome, found Ahmed Rashid in a state of extreme agitation.

Summers had expected it. How could it be any other way for the poor guy? Rashid was going through a hell Summers couldn't imagine. Summers' wife and kids were safe back in Green Bay, Wisconsin. He had done his time as a field agent in Third World hellholes during his early days with the agency. He'd seen enough dead bodies and grim doings to be jaded, yet the kidnap scene of slaughter where this guy's wife and son were taken from had been enough to shake Summers up all the more.

Rashid was a cultured man, normally of elegant bearing. That person was long gone. His hair was uncombed. His face was lined with deep, brooding crevices of worry. His eyes were wired with shock. His appearance, rumpled, disheveled.

Summers said, "I got over here fast as I could when they told me you'd changed your mind."

"I have. I'm returning to Syria. I'm sorry, Summers. You're good man doing a difficult job. But I see no choice. Would you feel any different if you were in my position?"

Summers wasn't about to go down *that* rabbit hole. He'd already turned the question over in his mind without satisfaction.

He said, "You're right about mine being a difficult job. Yes, as a man I empathize with you one hundred percent. I can't deny that, Rashid. But my job is to convince you not to go back. To stay here, helping us with what you know."

"I fear your task is impossible for you to carry out," said Rashid with sorrow in his voice. "You have what I've already given you. That surely will be of help."

"It will, but there's so much more"

"I understand. But it cannot be, Summers. They have my wife and son. They've threatened to kill them both unless I return and cease cooperating with you."

"You think they'll let you live once you're back, after what you've done?"

"My life is no longer my primary concern," said Rashid. "It is the life of my lovely Denise and my son, Ali. They are all that matter to me."

"And you think going back will save their lives? You're putting a lot of faith in the negotiations of terrorists."

"I'm going back," said Rashid. "This cannot go on. I cannot eat, I cannot sleep. Do you not see, Summers? If my Denise and Ali die at the hands of these terrorists, it will be because of *me*. No one else. Their blood would be on *my* hands. I have the choice of choosing between life and death for my family. I must choose life. There are no other options."

"There's one," said Summers. "His name is Jack Cody."

"The man been sent to rescue them? You told me there were complications."

"I don't have the details," Summers admitted, "but he and another agent are in country. Local assets will assist in the operation. The man has never failed before on a mission."

Rashid said, "I am sorry, Summers. You're wasting your time. My mind is made up," said Rashid. "I'm going back."

"But you're dealing with terrorists. They'll double-cross you. You'll end up dead and so will your wife and child. At least let's hold off to see what happens with Cody. You're not negotiating with terrorists here; you're dealing with the United states of America; everything it has and everything it represents. Ahmed, the only real hope for bringing your wife and son home alive is to give our two agents the chance to complete their mission."

"And if they die? What if they disappear and are never heard from again? What then, Summers?"

Summers sensed the first weakening in Rashid's resolve despite his words. It was, after all, a case of emotional versus rational. The poor man was ravaged by concern for his loved ones. But he could hardly refute the logic behind Rashid's words. Summers made some fast computations in his mind.

He said, "Give us six hours. Is that too much to ask?"

"You have much faith in this man, Cody."

"I do, and he's got solid backup."

Rashid considered the matter somberly, without speaking, for an entire minute. It felt like an eternity there in the silence between them.

Then Rashid said, "Very well. Six hours."

✳ ✳ ✳ ✳ ✳

In all of his ten years of life, Ali Rashid had never felt this alone. He lay with a thin sheet concealing the knife he held against his chest. The blade was so sharp he'd accidentally inflicted a tiny cut to his little finger. Hardly any blood but he considered it to be a warning to be most careful with this weapon he had taken from the terrorist who tried to molest his mother.

Majid, the man's name was. The way Majid glanced around the floor and under the bed after Ali snagged the knife from Majid's belt made Ali wonder if Majid would come to realize it was Ali who'd taken his knife. It should have been clear enough. But then Majid was clearly an inferior sort. What would happen if he thought things through and realized the likelihood of Ali now possessing his knife? He would confront Ali. What would happen when he found the knife?

Ali realized he lived life in a sheltered world thanks to the status of his parents. At the same time, thanks to the internet and gossip shared with the few friends he had at school, he knew of the world outside his bubble as well. And there were the video games he and his friends played. His mother didn't exactly approve when she overheard or happened to see some of the violent goings on involved in the games but he was never forbidden to play them. In the video games the bad guys and the violence were exciting.

The killing of the CIA agents in Rome, the kidnapping of Ali and his mother, had shaken Ali to his core. This wasn't exciting. It was real and tragic and scary.

Ali thought about his father. Was he alive? What was he doing to get Ali and his mother set free? They were human pawns, Ali and his mom; caught in a life and death game between Ali's father and the people his father had betrayed. Ali and his father had never been close. The business affairs of his father, and any disagreements between his mother and father, were never aired in front of Ali, who was hardly interested anyway. At this stage of his young life, Ali had enthusiasm only for video games, sports and the small circle of friends he'd made at the exclusive school he attended.

There was only one person Ali trusted. One person who was always there for him. He intended to use the knife to defend his mother if they ever came for her again; if they tried in any way to harm her.

Holding the knife there in the darkness somehow made him feel brave...while at the same time filling him with dread. He began to shiver though it was not cold. The shivering became an uncontrollable quaking, anxiety taking hold. He returned the knife to its hiding place, strapped to an ankle beneath the frock he wore.

Ali went into the next room and stood beside where his mother lay. He was surprised to find her awake, staring wide eyed at the ceiling.

Denise's gaze softened when she saw her little boy standing there beside her.

Ali found his voice.

"Mom...I'm cold."

For the first time in longer than she could remember, Denise Rashid's little man fell asleep in her arms that night. Though she still could not fall asleep, the rhythm of her child's steady breathing filled her with a determination not to give into despair.

They were going to make it; she and her son. Denise told herself that they would survive whatever was coming next.

* * * * *

A few hundred feet away, at the end of the narrow corridor, a room had been converted into Fared al-Hor's office, thus making it HQ for the operation. Abdul Kemal sat across the room, overhearing Fared's cell phone conversation with his superior in Damascus.

There was not much to overhear since the call apparently was to inform and instruct Fared. There was little to hear except for Fared's periodic acknowledgment of what he was hearing. There was likewise no way to read the stony mask that was Fared's cool countenance.

When the call was completed, Fared holstered his cell phone.

He said, "News from Deir ez-Zour."

He turned to part a curtain and stare at the tank and the

patrolling Hezbollah troopers outside under the night lights.

Kemal said, "A change in plans?"

As the architect of the Rashid kidnapping in Rome and the subsequent transportation of the hostages here to Iraq, Kemal had been thoroughly briefed on the force poised to attack the US Army position guarding the gas processing plant in Syria. The two actions were not otherwise connected except for the hidden hand of Syria directing both endeavors.

"Not a change of plans," said Fared, his expression stoic. "More of a complication."

"How so?"

"The attack on the gas plant will commence shortly, as scheduled," Fared told him. "That has not changed. We are, after all, dealing with RTL. Their central command in Russia brooks no delay or inefficiency. But there has occurred, I'm told, a disruption in the chain of command at Deir ez-Zour."

"That must have some relevance or they wouldn't call," said Kemal with a frown.

"We'll see. Pornov, the Russian, and Mahmoud have been assassinated," Fared told him. "Damascus has Mahmoud's replacement en route. Pornov has been replaced. Yes, a most efficient organization. But it is a complication worthy of concern."

"Assassinated, you say."

"Two sentries were also slain. There is evidence it was a work of a lone commando. That is why I've been contacted. Apparently there is an unknown element at work from the American side that we were not prepared for. This resulted in the elimination of Mahmoud and the Russian."

"A lone commando," mused Kemal. "And they suspect he'll show up here?" He gave a snort. "If there is only a single man who could take out four, he certainly must be formidable. But we are miles away and if he did all that from that American base and if the attack there is about to commence, he should certainly have enough to keep him occupied there, is that not so?"

"So it would seem," said Fared. "This concerns me only because it concerns Damascus. And these are Americans we are talking about. A formidable enemy."

"Has there been any word on Ahmed Rashid?"

"No. We have been instructed to remain vigilant against this unknown element. You will advise the Hezbollah commander outside of this."

Kemal nodded. He left the room to follow Fared's instruction.

Kemal's mind was busy. He'd followed his orders from Tehran. His part should be done and over with for all practical purposes. He had lived up to his reputation as a master planner, had he not? A man who could put a master plan into action such as the kidnapping of Denise Rashid and the child. It had gone so smoothly. He had much to be proud of; much to thank Allah for His grace. From Rome to this base at a deserted oasis in Iraq, the pace of the past day still had adrenaline pumping madly through his veins.

It was unfortunate; the matter of Majid molesting the woman. It saddened Kemal to think of it and so he didn't. One never knew the demons that might lurk within those befriended.

Fared had dealt with the matter fairly in Kemal's opinion and so he had dismissed it.

What concerned him was that while he should have already returned to his beloved Iran by now with the kidnapping successfully accomplished, here he was instead, cast in the role of babysitter; present only to watch over the hostages.

How would this end? Would the woman and her son live through tomorrow? That was up to Fared. Or more precisely, thought Kemal, it was up to Ahmed Rashid in Rome. Then there was the "unknown element" that Fared had referred to. But in truth, who lived and who died was in the hands of Allah alone.

The only other thing Kemal knew with certainty was that, should this supposed lone commando, the "unknown element," put in an appearance at this secluded oasis, he would find only the fires of Allah awaiting him.

CHAPTER FOURTEEN

The two Free Syrian Army soldiers were waiting for Cody when he returned to the base, having arrived in his absence.

Yavuz and Arjan.

The former was stocky, built close to the ground. Yavuz was a munitions expert. He wore a backpack which he patted affectionately and referred to as containing his "little toys." Cody nodded over his brief inspection of the assortment of high explosives and detonators. Arjan was a few years older, taller with less physical heft. They both looked meaner and tougher than hell. Each carried an assault rifle and wore a holstered pistol. They had the appearance of every Islamic fighting man Cody had seen in Syria: short beards, eyes that had seen it all, ready to kick ass at a moment's notice.

After a round of handshakes and introductions, Cody stepped off to the side with Larson.

The base CO hadn't yet gotten himself together. You could see it in his eyes; in the nervous, constant licking of dry lips.

There was the faint trace of beer on his breath.

Cody handed Larson the tablet and cell phone.

"Property of the late General Pornov."

"Pornov?"

"He was their commander."

"Was?"

Cody ignored the interruption.

"There will be plenty of useful info on the tablet and the phone. See that it gets to Lt. Col. Stratton in Qatar ASAP."

Larson tensed noticeably at having to take orders from a civilian. He took the items handed him and set them on his desk.

"I'll see to it," he said. "Do we know—"

Cody interrupted Larson, thinking of the time slipping away and two hostages needing to be rescued.

He said, "We'll know everything soon enough once Stratton's people start sifting and analyzing. It's a Russian private military outfit bankrolled by the Syrians. They're here to take this gas processing plant."

Larson paled visibly.

"Then they are going to attack us! Oh jeez, we are so screwed! You've seen the drone footage. We're vastly outnumbered, Cody. Vastly outnumbered! Why isn't Washington doing something? We're being served up for slaughter?"

The door opened. Sergeant Samuels step in.

"They're on the move," he reported. "The whole shebang are pulling around those trailers and houses and forming up like they're fixing to come straight this way. You'd better have a look, sir. We've got to get out word on this."

Larson sent Cody a frightened glance.

"You're from Washington. Big time mucky muck and all that. Can't you see we're about to be annihilated here? Can't you do something?"

"Get a hold of yourself, Captain." Cody kept his voice calm and even. "You've got Samuels and forty men who aren't about to back down. Neither can you. Get out there and do your damn job, mister."

Larson looked taken aback, buzzed on a beer high, not knowing whether to be frightened or pissed off. With his top sergeant waiting at the door, the CO reined in his reaction and broke eye contact. He hurried out with Samuels, leaving Cody alone with Sara.

She said, "I've taken what steps I could while you were gone. Sergeant Samuels had several recommendations for shoring up our defense perimeter. I gave him the go-ahead and we didn't bother asking the captain about it first."

Cody nodded in agreement. "We may have to go further than that with Larson."

"You mean relieve him of command?"

"We have that power if we need it. But right now let's shift gears. Have you been able to get anything out of the FSA guys?"

"Are you kidding?" Sara smiled. "This is not a region where women are deferred to. Those two have been eagerly awaiting your return with sealed lips."

"Then let's not keep them waiting."

"It's good we'll have them as backup," said Sara, "as long as they don't get in our way."

Cody cleared his throat. "Uh, they won't be getting in *our* way. You're staying here on base."

Sara's eyes narrowed. "Like hell I am. Cody, we were sent in to work as a team."

"And I was put in charge."

"So you're pulling rank."

"Women aren't deferred to in this region," he chided her with a mild grin to take the sting out. Serious again, he added, "Stop it. We don't have time. I'll bring the hostages directly here."

"Where I'll be waiting on the sidelines."

"Where you'll be keeping an eye on Larson," he corrected, "in case—or let's say for when—he goes completely off the rails."

"You want me to take command? The captain could be difficult."

"Samuels will back you up and so likely will every man on the base. Have Top get through to Stratton. Tell them what's at stake here and that it's going down. Tell him you want a direct connect to POTUS."

"I guess I'm not on the sidelines," said Sara. "Sorry, Cody."

When they rejoined the FSA men in the next room, the militia men had plenty of intel to share. No time was spent on amenities. Both men had some command of English, Yavuz more so than Arjan. So it was Yavuz who did the talking for them.

What it amounted to was that Mrs. Rashid and her son were being held by Iranian terrorists just across the Euphrates River in neighboring Iraq; held at an old and abandoned oasis guarded by ten Hezbollah troopers. They had a tank on loan from a nearby Iranian militia.

Those present at the oasis included the three who had carried out the kidnapping and the massacre of the CIA agents in Rome. Yavuz even supplied their names: the Iranians, Kemal and Majid, and their Syrian control, someone named Fared al-Hor. The hostages at present were thought to be alive and unharmed. Arjan produced a folded map and indicated the location of the oasis. They would be crossing the Euphrates, their travel time estimated to be about one hour.

Yavuz tried to explain something about a crazy man who lived in the desert, but the language barrier got in the way, and so the FSA man indicated he'd presented all he knew relevant to their mission.

After hearing them out, Cody said, "Can this intel be trusted? How does it come to you?"

"One of the Iranians, Majid, was seeing a woman who lived near here. His associates are not supposed to know. The woman has a cousin serving our cause. On a prior visit, Majid bragged to the woman of what they were about to do. It took longer than anticipated for word to reach us and be verified. But now we are here and now you know what we know. What is it we will do next, American?"

Cody said, "Let's get started."

They stepped outside.

The atmosphere of the base had changed during Cody's relatively short absence. When he and Sara first arrived, the small detachment had been abuzz with anticipation and preparation, vehicles and men seeming to move with a defined sense of purpose everywhere you looked, not unlike folks back home in the states preparing for the arrival of a tornado already sighted in the distance. The vibe now had shifted to that ominous, expectant silence right before the storm. Every preparation had been made. The soldiers and equipment were in place along the perimeter. Cody picked up on a sort of "bring it on" vibe.

The FSA men had come with their own transportation plus a third in tow for him. Three side-by-sides, which Cody had seen on his way in, awaited them. Three Trailmaster Challenger 300E rough country vehicles, each equipped with a roll cage. Arjan bragged in his broken English about the souped-up engines he'd worked on that would far exceed the vehicles' standard speed limit of 50 mph, along with hydraulic disc brakes and a few other modifications to improve mobility. Each of them was armed with an M4 carbine strapped across their back, a sidearm, a bandolier of spare magazines for each weapon, and a combat knife sheathed at mid-chest.

Captain Larson and Sergeant Samuels stood nearby. Cody and Sara walked over to join them while the FSA guys prepped the side-by-sides.

As they crossed the distance, Cody entertained a momentary flashback to one of his favorite movies, *High Noon*; a movie he hadn't seen in years but knew well. In that film, a sense of waiting for the other shoe to drop prevailed throughout; the lawman and the townspeople, everybody waiting for the train to arrive because the train was bringing the bad guys and when they arrived, all hell would break lose. Everyone knew, everyone could feel, the energy building up for that imminent explosion. That was the vibe that prevailed tonight on this little base in the Syrian desert.

Larson had his binoculars again and was staring through them in the direction of the vacated community. From this distance, the activity way over there consisted mostly of pinpoints of light moving about accompanied by the vague but unmistakable rumble of the trucks and tanks in the otherwise silent desert night.

Samuels gave Cody and Sara a nod in greeting as they approached. He said, "Looks like we're in for it."

Sara indicated the weaponry and men dug in along the perimeter. "We're as ready for them as we'll ever be."

"We?" Larson sneered and nodded his head at the side-by-sides. "Looks like the two of you are leaving before the fun begins."

Cody said, "I'm leaving. Ms. Durell will continue to bless this base with her presence."

Sergeant Samuels registered concern. "You sure you want to stick around, ma'am? It's going to get mighty hot any time now."

"You men have your job," said Sara. "I have mine."

Larson couldn't seem to wipe the sneer off his face or from his voice. He said, "You're crazy. If we don't get some help soon, we're all going to die." He lowered the binoculars and handed them to Cody. "Here," he said. "See for yourself."

Cody took the NVD and had his look.

Considering the foot journey he had just made covering the distance both ways, it was like looking along his own backtrack. And yeah, things *had* changed in the brief time since his return and *not* for the good.

In the greenish glow of the NVD binoculars, he clearly discerned the convoy of troop carriers, each one jam packed with mercs, advancing at a slow but steady pace, accompanied by the tanks.

Cody passed the NVD to Sara. He said, "I'll be back as soon as I can."

Larson made an unpleasant sound in his throat. "Come back to what? Look at that firepower! We'll be nothing more than a smudge on the earth within the next hour. You're picking a hell of a time to run out on us."

Samuels started to protest.

"Sir—"

Sara beat him to it, staring daggers at the CO. "We're here to do *our* job, Captain, not yours."

Cody said, "You'll excuse me. A woman and a little boy being held hostage are waiting on me. I'm gone."

He stalked off in the direction of the FSA men and their vehicles. Sara kept pace with him.

"That Larson, what an asshole."

"Right as usual," said Cody. "He's the reason I want you here. Don't hesitate if he loses it completely."

"I'm on it," she assured him.

"If that tablet and cell phone I brought back are still on his desk, see that they're securely locked away until we can get them to Stratton."

"Trust me," Sara said. "I'll keep them with me."

Cody felt a surge of the affection he felt for her; he usually compartmentalized it away from their work. But sometimes…

"I've always trusted you," said Cody. "I always will."

He was a man who'd never paid much, if any, attention to romance. He'd dated, of course. He enjoyed the company of intelligent, beautiful women. But he'd been too doggone busy with sports, studies and career goals to have time for anything else.

When love did claim Cody and they began a family, a romantic nature within him had surfaced. He'd loved domestic life. He adored his wife and children and when they were stolen from him in that fiery bomb explosion meant to kill him, he'd lost everything and he only wanted to die so they could be together again. The shrink called it "survivor guilt," but giving it a name did not change how the felt.

That's what losing his wife, his children—everyone he truly loved—had done to him. It was only time and his spiritual recovery, thanks to the healing power of this woman, Sara, that had brought him back from the abyss.

Romance?

They were friends at the deepest level. As a team they'd been through combat together, the stuff that truly bonds when your survival depends on the one covering your back. This breeds a level of trust that runs deeper than you'll find in many marriages. Ask any cop or soldier. This woman in his arms had brought him back from hell. The grieving, suicidal person they still called Suicide Cody really was no more, thanks to Sara Durell.

Romance?

They were lovers when time and circumstance provided the opportunity. Given the nature of their work and their commitment to never letting their personal feelings for each other get in the way of that work, a confluence of time and place was rare indeed.

He and Sara were halfway between the waiting side-by-side vehicles and where Larson and Samuels remained occupied with what was happening in the distance. When no one was looking, Cody drew Sara into the deepest shadows he could find.

Their arms went around each other. The embrace was so close and lasted for so many heartbeats, eyebrows would have been raised had there been witnesses.

Sara whispered between kisses, "Be careful out there tonight, big man."

He whispered in her ear, "It's a promise. Keep an eye on things until I get back."

One final kiss, lasting longer than those preceding it. Sara stepped away, breaking their embrace. She said, "Do what you have to, Cody. Just come back safe, hear? And we'll pick up where we left off."

The romance, the promise, in those words was as good a parting as any. With the heat that burned between them, it was hard to believe they'd only stolen little more than a minute for this intimate clinch. When they left those shadows, they were again striding shoulder to shoulder to rejoin the FSA men.

Arjan spent less than a minute acquainting Cody with the

side-by-side and the modifications he'd made. There had been occasions in during Cody's years of service when a mission required the acquisition of new skills. Consequently, he'd had training in everything from flying a helicopter to racing a speedboat to maneuvering a tank to riding a camel, the last being the one skill he'd yet to master. The side-by-side was a piece of cake.

The rough terrain vehicles fired up, drawing the attention of some of the soldiers along the perimeter.

Captain Larson remained staring into the distance through his binoculars, transfixed, unable to draw himself away.

Sergeant Samuels crossed over to stand beside Sara, bearing witness to the moment. There was a round of thumbs up.

Then Cody and the pair of FSA militiamen tore off into the night.

CHAPTER FIFTEEN

In the White House, President Harwood met off the record with his closest advisors in a cramped basement facility called the Situation Room. A high-tech, highly secure facility once reserved for managing the occasional world crisis, these days it was in almost constant use. The Situation Room had lately become one of the busiest parts of the West Wing.

The president sat at the head of a conference table. At his right hand sat Corbett, Chief of Staff and trusted friend. Also present were the Secretary of Defense, the Secretary of State, the Director of the Central Intelligence Agency, and the National Security Advisor.

Calhoun, the CIA Director, was a pale-skinned man in a dark suit. He was known for having a computer-like mind. He spoke crisply.

"Thanks to the information that's been passed along to us by Sara Durell, the BG on our mystery outfit has fallen into place."

The president nodded his satisfaction. "Cody walks away with it from a soft intel probe and finds a way to expedite it home. Damn, do those two make for a dynamic duo or what?"

"Setting up direct contact link with them via satellite was a good move, sir."

"We've been drilling the Russians for info since that outfit was spotted crossing the Euphrates," said Harwood. "Cody takes it into his head to find out on his own. So now we know." His fists clenched. He grimaced. "Another one of those damn private military outfits. Now what the hell?"

"They belong to the RTL Group," said Calhoun. "The initials of some obscure Soviet general. Their financing comes from a syndicate of prominent Russian military contractors. RTL is a global mercenary operation not registered as a legal entity anywhere in the world."

"Just like the Wagner Group," said the president, his grimace frozen in place. "Those bastards have been raising hell over in the Ukraine. These private armies muck things up but good. Now that the beast has a name, what's the word from Moscow?"

"Same as with the Wagner Group," said Calhoun, his expression glum. "The Kremlin claims they have no control over groups like Wagner and RTL."

"They're lying," said Glen MacDonald with a scowl. The Secretary of State affected a rumpled appearance at odds with his proven, hard-nosed mastery of international diplomacy. "This bunch is damn straight operating under Kremlin authorization. Moscow has increasingly been turning to groups like RTL to expand their global reach. They hire out to countries as well as to regional warlords throughout Asia and the Mideast."

"If the Russians are lying," said the president, "the intent is pretty damn obvious."

MacDonald nodded agreement.

"The Kremlin is using RTL to test our willingness to defend and maintain a presence in Syria."

J. Lansdale, the Secretary of Defense, growled, "It's Lenin's maxim. Test the opponent with a bayonet, going forward if he finds mush and stopping if he finds steel." Lansdale was a stocky man, brusque in appearance and manner. He tugged irritably at an earlobe. "This punk bunch is up to no damn good, sir. We should preempt the sons of bitches. They want a fight? Let's open fire and give 'em a taste. They'll back off."

Latisha Freeman, the National Security Advisor, leaned earnestly forward in her chair. A middle-aged African American, Freeman's background in the military and academic arenas had marked her with a no-nonsense, plainspoken style.

"The stakes in this game are too high," she said. "We need to keep all lines of communication open. I strongly advise caution and restraint, Mister President, unless we are first fired upon. A communication snafu in the field right now could result in war if we were to attack a Russian outfit conducting a training exercise."

"When you're right, Latisha," said the president, "you're right all the way. That's the way we'll let it stand for now. Thank you for your input, everyone. Hang loose tonight. This is going down in real time and if it blows up, it will happen tonight."

When the others had filed out, Harwood noticed the small

smile worn by Jim Corbett, who sat appraising him from his seat at the conference table.

"What is it, Jim?"

"Just thinking."

"Well, there's nothing wrong with that. But from a best friend, it's an evasive reply."

"Uh, okay. Here it is then. I guess inside I was admiring that masterful performance I just sat through."

"Oh?"

"Don't forget, Mister President, we're best friends, you and I, because of all those hard-fought campaigns that got us where we are. Sir, I know your moves. I'm just saying I admire your skill with that bunch."

"They're the best people we could find for their jobs."

"Of course they are," said Corbett. "I helped you pick them, remember? And I just spent the past thirty minutes watching you politely listen to each one of with what I know to be an open mind."

"And?"

"And after you heard them out," said Corbett, "you stayed the course you've been on all along. That takes some doing when you're going up against those four. At least three of them would just as soon you said bombs away and ended it right here and now. Freeman's your ace in the hole. If she wasn't on your side, you'd be odd man out."

"Yes, but I'd still be the president," said Harwood. "I'm not up against anyone on *our* team, Jim. It's the goddamn barbarians out there, the ones who won't be satisfied until they've torn

down every last piece of what we call decency and civilization."
Harwood's eyes grew steely. He thumped the table with a fist
"Kidnapping a woman like Mrs. Rashid and her child. Makes
my stomach turn."

"That's what we have to keep sight of," said Corbett. "It all
ties together, doesn't it?"

The president nodded. "I will not allow us to become *like*
those we want to take down."

"I get it," Corbett said. "I'm with you all the way, you know
that. Latisha was right. We'll handle whatever comes our way.
America always has and always will prevail. But we're not about
to strike the first blow."

"It's good to have you on my side, Jim," said the president.
"And you're right. I was listening to my advisors with open ears.
All of those viewpoints coming in at once made me realize
something else."

"Cody," said Corbett.

"That's right. Cody."

"I'm onto you there, too, you know."

"Oh?"

"You didn't order Cody to make that soft probe. You didn't
have to."

"It was too dangerous and not the primary mission."

"That's true. But you knew Cody would take the initiative
and make that probe on his own."

"And now we know how deep the shit is that we've sent him
and Durell into," said the president. "A flare-up that could lead
to World War III and a hostaged woman and her child. This is

a suicide mission if there ever was one."

"God help them all," said Corbett.

The president exhaled a long sigh.

He said, "I hope God's up to it."

CHAPTER SIXTEEN

The Euphrates is the longest and most important river in the Middle East. Originating in Turkey, it flows through Syria and Iraq. In the Bible (Genesis 24:14) a river named Euphrates is one of the four rivers that flow from the Garden of Eden. The Euphrates was the source of major civilizations like those of the Sumerians and Mesopotamians, and holds great importance to the civilizations of the area in modern times.

Crossing the river was one of the details of this mission that had been left to the FSA since the destination was not known until Yavuz and Arjan brought that new intel with them. Most bridges crossing the river were under Syrian control while others in this remote region were held by rebel militias both of the FSA and ISIS. It was that sort of a battleground.

Yavuz took point once the three side-by-sides left the American base, followed by Cody and then Arjan. The convoy wended their way through the darkness, across hard top soil, over small rocks and rough, broken ground. The side-by-sides were designed and built for terrain such as this useless land, wholly unsuitable for human habitation. A night-shrouded world of desolation and tumbled rocks; scattered limestone, some the size of boulders though most of the trail Yavuz guided them along was pebbly.

The air cooled, not by much but noticeably, as they made a mild, gradual descent into the Euphrates Valley. There were stunted juniper trees growing among the boulders and traces of scattered scrub vegetation, though in general the terrain remained deeply scarred, pitted by centuries of merciless sun and violent sand storms.

Yavuz led them to a desolate place along the river. At its bank, the waterway that in its glory rivaled the mighty Mississippi back home, was along this stretch no more than ankle deep.

During the last two decades, the Euphrates had been continually drying up due to drought and water mismanagement. The Book of Revelations prophecies its drying up as a sign of the End Times. The Koran prophesies that the river drying up will reveal unknown treasures that will cause strife and war.

In the here and now, it made for an easy crossing.

Beyond the river, the terrain gradually grew into hills that became larger and larger until they were huge masses of granite and limestone, their slopes covered with loose rock and shale. The world was limned in the silvery light of the quarter moon.

So it was with some surprise that he rounded a corner, Arjan behind and just to his left, and collided with a wall of light.

He hit the brakes, slamming the side-by-side to a halt. *Damn!*

Those lights were blinding! Cody squinted, raising one gloved hand to shade his vision as he fought to discern the shapes of whatever it was out there beaming all those lumens, but it was pointless. Whatever they were shining at him emitted the same power as a spotlight's beam—halogen-hard, bright and blinding. He forced himself to look away, waiting for the spots dancing in his eyes to fade.

A voice cried out in Arabic—a single word. The light dimmed sufficiently for Cody to make out the figures of men on horseback. He knew pockets of Sunni tribesmen traveled the porous border between Iraq and Syria. And he knew them to be fine horsemen and worthy fighters. This area of Syria was ruled principally by warlords. It seemed he, Arjun and Yavuz had stumbled upon a clutch of them.

Cody studied the men. They were a lean, hard-faced bunch. Even the elders, who looked to be in their sixties and seventies, looked vicious enough to give a young man a tough go in a knife fight. Indeed, curved blades in brass sheaths adorned many a belt of the hooded robes the riders wore. Some sported *keffiyeh* around their necks and a few still had the hoods pulled forward on their riding cloaks. They had obviously been traveling through the desert themselves, their caravan brought to an abrupt stop by the audible whine of the side-by-sides' micro-engines approaching.

So, they set up their spotlight and waited, Cody thought, and nervously eyed the nearest group's hardware. The man sitting a-horsed closest to him gripped the frame of a well-oiled FN assault rifle while the warriors to either side clutched HK machine pistols. For a bunch of guys out on a trail ride, these *hombres* looked ready to take on a Syrian patrol or Iraqi bandit hoard. But the biggest shock was yet to come.

"Clear a path, *muchachos!*"

The crowd of horsemen parted and a lone figure emerged. Sitting astride a vast white horse, he was a big man festooned in a Stetson, birch-bark patterned vest and the most elaborate set of embroidered chaps Cody had seen this side of a Montana rodeo. The rider did not so much resemble a man portraying Roy Rogers as an exaggerated parody of a man portraying Roy Rogers, with all the fabulous get-up and glamor of an old-timey silent movie star. Cody half expected the action to break and a scene card to drop with the words *OUR HERO* emblazed on it in elaborate script.

Who the hell do we have here? he wondered with a stab of morbid fascination.

"Well, howdy pilgrim," the cowboy apparition intoned, touching his hat brim and speaking perfect cowboy lingo in Arabic-accented English. Cody thought he could detect the barest trace of Oxford there, too. "You'd be a long way from your spread, I reckon, *inshallah*. Far enough away. And over the line to mine."

Cody peered around. He saw no fences or boundary markers but knew this far into the desert it didn't matter. Here was a man with a dozen-strong cavalry at his back saying this was his land. Cody saw no reason to argue.

"We were unaware of whose territory we'd entered." He inclined his head respectfully. "Mister, ah...?"

"I am Zahran ibn-Zahran al-Sahiri. You may address me as *sheikh*. But my men call me *rayiys*, pilgrim. That means boss. Like on a cattle drive. I reckon you can understand that lingo, *sahib*."

The man spoke in the most confusing gibberish—a mix of perfect English interspersed with the kind of cornball dialogue Cody associated with B westerns. This Zahran was obviously western educated but somehow now found himself in the position of a tribal warlord, riding herd over a patch of desert that was politically fluid and treacherous, leading his own personal cavalry while wearing cowboy duds. In the bleak and violent wasteland of war-torn Syria it was wildly absurd.

"I get you." Cody allowed his statement to end on a severe down inflection, wishing very much to convey displeasure. He and his friends were busy. They were in haste. They had no time for niceties. But the hint, if intended for Zahran ibn-Zahran, went completely unnoticed.

"So, because yonder is my spread—" The cowboy threw a hand in a vaguely southerly direction "—I reckon you understand if I ask you to respect my property and go around. No man shall let another walk on his patrimony, *makhtoub-brebi* if you catch my drift there, pardner?"

Cody frowned. "Look. We really have to cut through. We're prepared to compensate you. Pay you for the inconvenience..."

"Money? *Money?*" The man climbed down from the saddle and strode out into the clearing between his horsemen and Cody's side-by-side. "You think this is about *money*, pilgrim? Nosiree, *inshallah*. This is about a man's ranch. His castle. His dignity. You cannot pass because I say you cannot. And if my word is not law upon my own land, then what am I?"

Cody had to admit that the man was making perfect sense. Indeed, what was a man whose word meant nothing in his homeland? But they were burning daylight. And he had a job to do.

"Tell you what," Cody offered. "What say you we solve this the old fashioned way? You and me. *Mano a mano.* No weapons. Just our fists. If you win, I go around. If I win, my companions and I pass through. What do you say?"

Cody studied Zahran as he considered this offer. The desert warlord was a big man, broad-shouldered, barrel chested, with hands like paddles, and he carried himself with the pride and swagger of a leader unaccustomed to giving ground on even the smallest issues. For a moment, Cody thought the man might deploy some verbal trickery or the firepower inherent in the hands of his men. But after a long moment, he appeared to digest the challenge with a slow nod.

"Okay, pardner," he said, glancing back at his horse and stretching. "That's a fair offer. A courageous one, truthfully. You can take comfort in your bravery once I've beaten you to a pulp, *inshallah.*"

Cody watched as the warlord laid aside his assault rifle and removed his gun belt, handing both to a subaltern. Cody unholstered and put aside his own sidearm, then moved forward into the open space between the snout of his side-by-side and the phalanx formed by the horsemen. Zahran waited, hands on his hips, a bright grin beaming through his ragged beard.

"So!" He waved his arms. "You want to do this?"

Cody said nothing. Merely squared up and waited.

Zahran turned to his men. "Now you will see!" he cried. "Even against trained soldiers with modern equipment, our clan is stronger! It is because of our faith! *Inshallah!*"

With that, he whirled and came at Cody, fists swinging.

CHAPTER SEVENTEEN

For a big man, Zahran could sure move fast. Cody was forced to backpedal and bring his forearms together in front of his face to ward off blows. Even glancing off of the bones of his forearms, Zahran's punches hurt. When the next one came, Cody dodged it, lunged right, then left. He drove three quick blows into Zahran's ribs before backing away, his guard up.

The warlord went to one knee, breath leaving his body in a loud exhale. A murmur arose from his men. Hearing it, Zahran rallied and pushed himself back upright. He was still in the fight.

Cody didn't give him an opportunity to get set but went immediately on the attack. He took two long steps, then sent a flying kick Zahran's way. It connected with the warlord's hip, driving him back. Cody landed, set his stance and then kicked again, landing a blow on the same spot, causing Zahran to stagger. The man was having a hard time remaining upright. Cody sped in and hit him twice in the face, hard. Zahran recoiled, lost balance and dropped to his knees.

Cody paused. The man was down on all fours and panting heavily. Now seemed like a good time to offer him a graceful way out.

"You had enough?" he asked. "You want to...?"

A spray of sand and pebbles hit his face, launched from Zahran's right fist. The warlord roared as he sprang to his feet, following up his distraction with a full frontal assault. Kicks, slaps, swinging elbows and fists; they all collided with Cody's guard as he backed away, enduring the onslaught. He could hear Zahran's breath at close quarters, now–a rasping, groaning wheeze filled with anger and determination and...

Fatigue, Cody thought. *He's gassing out.*

Cody played it cool, enduring Zahran's attack, counting the blows until they began to slow. Three kicks became two, became lone punches, became widely spaced punches. Which told Cody the big man was getting tired, backing off and allowing himself a chance to rest...

So Cody lunged, taking a blow on the chest and another on the shoulder as he flashed forward, one hand fisted and the other held in knife-hand, fingers bunched and tensed as he drove them into Zahran's neck.

The warlord's cry was choked off and both hands went to his throat. A few more pounds of pressure and Cody would have shattered his Adam's apple, but he had deliberately softened the blow, seeking only to temporarily restrict Zahran's breathing. He appeared to have been successful. The warlord's expression of resolve wavered and the eyes beneath the brim of the Stetson grew watery.

"I…" The warlord raised a hand. *"I…"*

"You *what?"* Cody snarled.

Zahran lined up for one last punch, swung and keeled over to land face first in the sand. Cody gazed down at the prone body.

Zahran was done.

He turned to the assembled horsemen. "You heard him," he said. "If I win, we get to pass through. Are we going to have a problem?"

One of the men apparently spoke English. He translated Cody's words to the group and they responded by backing away from him and parting to clear a space for the side-by-sides. Cody went to his, taking up his gun belt and assault rifle and resecuring them as two of Zahran's men rushed forward to help their stricken warlord rise from the sand. The big man accepted their help until he stood upright, then shook off their hands as he stretched and turned to Cody.

"You won, *sahib."* He said this without a trace of embarrassment. "Good fighting, good tactics. Pilgrim, you're a gunslinger. A true warrior crusader, *inshallah.* I reckon we ain't seen your like since the days of Saladin, peace be upon him."

By Cody's reckoning, the distance between Saladin and the frontier America of Zahran's imagination was something on the order of five whole centuries. But he decided to let historical details go for now. He had won the day, secured passage for himself and his two escorts, and they were on track to their destination. Quibbling about dates seemed a waste of time just now.

"Thank you," Cody said quietly.

"No need for thanks," Zahran said, coughing out some of the dust he had swallowed upon hitting the ground. "You took what's yours. My men will offer you not problems. You are safe while in our territory. Nobody will harm you. You have my word."

"Good enough," Cody said, and started his side-by-side.

Again with Yavuz taking point, the three vehicles continued on. The bright lights behind them were extinguished.

The moon-washed hilly contours of the North Arabian Desert frontier became hardened, jagged spikes as Cody and the FSA men plunged into massive hillocks of granite. They had been surfing a smooth ocean of pebble and sand but soon were navigating a torturous goat path.

The night remained soundless except for their engine sounds which were in part muted by some muffler work done by Arjan who had also rigged each side-by-side with an odometer. Cody's odometer clocked 25 miles precisely when Yavuz executed a sharp right turn without slackening speed into a wadi, or ravine. On either side the high slanted walls of the wadi loomed overhead.

Cody cast an appraising glance left and right, relaxing when he noted how the unforested inclines left their approach completely exposed. There could be no ambush lurking up top that he would not spot ahead of time.

Steering was tricky speeding through the wadi, dodging large rocks, catching twists and turns of the winding riverbed sometimes on two wheels. Keeping up with Yavuz would have been death-defying in broad daylight! It occurred to Cody that it was moments like this that had earned him his nickname.

They continued on for just under another mile and rounded a particularly abrupt curve. Yavuz parked his side-by-side, killed his engine. Cody and Arjan joined him, following suit. Without engine noise, the desert night again became soundless.

They left the vehicles. Yavuz pointed to the right. "Over there."

He led the way to the wall of the wadi. A gully in the slope was almost perpendicular, a depression slightly larger than a 15-foot-wide ditch. To reach the top, they would have to climb nearly one-hundred feet.

Yavuz slapped his chest. "Is good exercise," he enthused. He started climbing.

Arjan and Cody exchanged a man to man glance of amusement at the younger man's energy, then, with rifles slung across their backs, they commenced climbing.

The climb took them the better part of an hour. Arduous but not daunting, the climb brought nearly every muscle into play. It was all about leverage and balance in addition to physical stamina. The FSA men had been well chosen for this mission. They matched Cody's stamina and strength. They reached the top as a team, tested and ready for more.

The top was little more than a small plateau cluttered with enormous granite and limestone boulders partially covered with chalky dust. Behind them was the top of the opposite wall of the wadi. In every other direction were more hills of limestone and granite.

They crawled on hands and knees to take up position behind a cluster of enormous boulders. From there it was easy enough to view the oasis encampment in the distance. The oasis was situated on a low plain; a quiet, sleepy tableau dozing beneath the black, star-studded dome of night.

Through his NVD binoculars, Cody could clearly make out a 10-foot-high wall surrounding what had no doubt once been a sumptuous desert hideaway. Now it was occupied by the Iranian Hezbollah unit Yavuz had told him about. And there was the tank, a Russian T-54 with a 140-millimeter cannon.

Cody studied the layout, noting each feature. In the center of the camp was the main building, a low, immense square stone structure that was well lit and patrolled by a pair of rifle bearing sentries. Off to the side, a line of smaller structures where the off duty troopers would be sleeping. In front of the low stone building sat a Jeep-like command car. Further along stood a small collection of vehicles: a couple of Jeep-like vehicles, each with an M-60 mounted on its back, and a pair of personnel carriers for transporting the troops.

From these observations could be drawn a likely estimate of no more than a dozen Hezbollah soldiers present.

As Cody's eyes and mind were committing the layout to memory, a man stepped from the front of the stone house. He simply stood there, smoking a cigarette as if in contemplation. The guy's eyes swept the outlying terrain.

For a few passing seconds, the man and Cody would have made eye contact but for the distance separating them and the veil of night.

Cody lowered the compact NVD, replacing it in its thin carrying case which he pocketed. He and the FSA fighters crawled to the rear of the boulders, to the side that could not be seen by anyone below.

"You see," whispered Yavuz, "it is as we were told. They have security, yes. But they are not expecting trouble. Half their force is asleep."

"Looks that way," said Cody. "The woman and child will be in the stone house."

"I agree with you," said Yavuz.

"We think as one; the three of us," said Arjan. He spoke with a solemn certainty. "This will be a good fight."

Yavuz eyed Cody.

"And so, American, we have led you here. We are ready, Arjan and I. What is next?"

"Now we get 'er done," growled Cody.

He moved out, one militiaman to either side. The team of three advanced on the dozing oasis.

✳ ✳ ✳ ✳ ✳

Fared al-Hor stood in front of the stone house that dominated the oasis. It felt fine to be standing out here in the desert night, smoking his cigarette, taking in the pure night air.

The sentries marched past him. Young men with their eyes lowered respectfully, the rifles held close over the shoulder; left hand bracing the rifle in place by its strap, right hand across the chest, close to the trigger.

Fared nodded to himself. Kemal had done as instructed, tightening discipline in the ranks. The Iranian soldiers here at the oasis understood that it was Fared who was their control officer, not their Iranian unit commander.

It is a good feeling to have, thought Fared. Not only for the sense of power it brought him, which was worth everything in and of itself, but also gaining the approval of his superiors in Damascus. All would go well here tonight, he assured himself, and when tonight was over and done he would return to Damascus to bask in his due: money, promotion and, yes—more power.

Despite the hour he felt wide awake and energized. He should have been exhausted, having been awake and active since the action in Rome nearly twenty hours earlier. Instead, he felt exhilarated, unable to relax. His mind couldn't stop racing, leapfrogging from one unrelated subject to another, seeming to gain momentum when he should have been slowing down like everyone around him. It was, after all, well past midnight.

He'd decided to step outside for a smoke, to see if the night air might relax him. It didn't. He was willing to accept that. And what did it matter, one sleepless night? His racing mind should be allowed to run free, shouldn't it? Examining. Reviewing. Applying every instinct within him to the furtherance of his ambitions and plans. So much was happening tonight. He would find time for sleep when the drama of this night had passed.

He stared off in the general direction of where, miles away in Syria, the RTL Group was about to stage its action. *How would things be going for them*, he wondered. He considered again the death of General Pornov. And there was the warning from Damascus that Pornov's death could be an indication of troubles to come for Fared's operation.

Fared assured himself they were safe enough here at this oasis. How could the enemy learn of this location? Abdul Kemal was a mastermind of this sort of setup with many terrorist actions to his credit. And the truckload of troopers from Tehran was likewise well armed and adequately trained. Yes, he assured himself, the oasis was well fixed; its defenses adequate.

Then there was Majid.

Fared frowned at the thought. With ops such as this, the Majids of the world always found a place. Thugs. Brutes. They came from the lower classes. The incident of Majid with the American woman still troubled Fared. It was too late to change course now, though. He'd already made his decision regarding the fellow. Majid was part of the equation. But he would never be used again.

The defection of Ahmed Rashid had set in motion one sequence of events while the RTL action in Syria led to another. The fact that Damascus was behind both did not mean the two threads need intersect. Fared would prefer they didn't. That would complicate everything.

He threw away the cigarette, his fingers warm from having smoked it down to a nub. He returned to his makeshift office in the stone house. There was only one aspect of the operation he did not look forward to.

That was the execution of the woman and the boy.

CHAPTER EIGHTEEN

Dimitri Volkov, packed in like a sardine with the other mercenaries in the troop carrier, felt a chill to the marrow of his bones despite the warm desert night. He had learned early that no man in the RTL Group ever made a suggestion or said please. When it was decreed time to board the troop carriers, the squad leaders began snarling and shouting profane commands, ordering every man to get off his butt and get on the damn trucks.

After weeks of relative inactivity, it was the combatant cliché of hurry up and wait. Now, the waiting was over. There was shoving, pushing and cursing as Dimitri and the rest of the mercenary fighters boarded the waiting troop carriers. The trucks rolled out as soon as each was loaded to capacity.

Dimitri had found himself the object of intense scrutiny and interrogation following the murder of General Pornov and the two sentries found outside Pornov's HQ. Dimitri had recovered from the intruder's punch behind his ear to find himself in a chair, barraged by questions Colonel Niktov, who assumed command following Pornov's demise.

Much to Dimitri's relief, they believed him. And why shouldn't they? He had the bruise behind his ear to prove his story. In the end, they threw him back into the ranks with the other mercs, waiting for the order to move out. Under ordinary circumstances, Dimitri would have been the object of considerable interest to his fellow fighters. But he was not. They were all focused on waiting for the order to board the trucks.

When the order came, when the pushing and shoving and men packed in tightly was complete, the troop carriers began moving forward.

For men who had spent the recent past engaged in little more than lounging about and bantering, there was no chitchat whatsoever among the men riding with Dimitri. They all understood that they were now approaching their moment of truth. The RTL mission was going down. Even the death of Pornov had not affected its implementation. That had to be on every man's mind. Who killed Pornov? No one had an answer for that one.

Dimitri only felt gratitude to the intruder who had spared him. That was a secret Dimitri would never reveal. But the thought remained: was Pornov's death an omen of ill fortune to come? That was the question that chilled Dimitri to the marrow.

After a short while the trucks were slowing. Then they drew to a stop. The squad leaders began snarling and shouting again, ordering every man off. On the ground they were organized, grouped facing the US military detachment ahead next to the gas plant. Around them the tanks were rumbling into position.

Dimitri felt like making a run for it. But where would he go? His squad leader would blow his brains out within a few steps as promised in that RTL recruitment talk. There was nowhere to go except face the objective. And what was that? It wasn't Africa this time. It wasn't the Ukraine. Were they about to take on the United States of America? The gossip in the ranks was that a bluff was being played. Dimitri hoped such was the case.

The squad leaders ordered them to check their weapons and prepare to advance.

$$* * * * *$$

In the operations section of the Al Udeid Air Base in Qatar, Lieutenant-Colonel Stratton stood behind a Specialist Fifth Class who was seated at her computer terminal, one in a long row of computer screens being monitored. Stratton was looking over her shoulder, watching the streaming satellite feed on her screen.

Stratton's gut had been tightening for the past thirty minutes, ever since the satellite feed began showing movement on the ground in Syria. He'd been able to contain his reaction to what he was witnessing on the feed but finally the need to vent got the best of him. He said, "Do you see what I see?"

The Spec 5 was startled at first. She'd been aware of Stratton's looming presence behind her, of course. But they hadn't spoken. She'd been intently watching her screen, typing in data that would accompany the images for all those viewing it. She was serious and intently focused. Her eyes never left the screen. She said, "Yes, sir. It looks like," she paused to study the feed a moment longer before continuing, "it looks like they're preparing to attack."

"Washington's getting this feed?"

"Yes, sir. The Pentagon and the White House."

"Well, hell."

Stratton bit his tongue. What good would it do to sound off, venting his tension and irritability? This young Spec 5 was as concerned about the situation as he was! He looked around the long, low-ceiling room. His eyes settled on Major Sawyer, the man in charge here.

Sawyer was a sturdily built, middle-aged black man, highly competent. He was watching the feed come in on the main video screen mounted high on a wall. He did not look happy. He nodded when Stratton approached.

"Sir."

Stratton's eyes also went to the big screen.

"Am I mistaken, Major, or are we about to see the shit hit the fan?"

"Looks that way, don't it, sir?"

"The specialist over there tells me the big shots in DC are all watching this along with us. Any idea, Major, why we're not blowing the hell out of that bunch of trouble seekers?"

Sawyer grunted his dissatisfaction. "Something about not wanting to fire the first shot of World War III," he said. "We made contact with the Russian military high command in country. It's like we were waking them up in the middle of the night. We've impressed upon them the severity of the situation on the ground and have urged them to stop the advance."

Stratton snorted.

"Right, just like we have since this damn thing began." His frustration put ice in every word. "Same with all of our diplomatic initiatives. Moscow stonewalling us, insisting they have nothing to do with it. Bullshit."

"That's the word, all right," Sawyer agreed. "But I'll wager they're feeling the same way in Washington, sir. Uh, I voted for President Harwood. I don't think he's going to let this go too much further without stepping in. That's when we'll get the green light."

"I just hope that's not too late for our boys," said Stratton.

"We're all praying for that, sir," said Sawyer.

Stratton could think of nothing to say in response to that, so he said nothing. He left the operations center.

He needed a break. He needed a cigarette. And he hadn't smoked in years! He denuded a stick of gum and stuck in his mouth. He began chomping savagely. Hell yeah, he needed a break. A break from sitting on the sidelines.

Stratton stood there outside the HQ building, surrounded by the sounds and atmosphere of the well-lit air base around him, busy even at this hour, taking a few minutes to gather his thoughts. He had to repress the combative energy coursing through him. He tried to think of something positive to quell the restlessness within him.

The dual image of Jack Cody and Sara Durell came to mind.

Had it only been hours ago when they met in his office and he briefed them on the situation that was endangering their mission? He'd been impressed with the rep those two had even before they'd met. And now, after spending even that short time making their acquaintance and with the knowledge of what their mission entailed, his admiration and respect for them had grown beyond measure. That same respect and admiration extended to the forty men entrenched against that sizable RTL force apparently poised to take them on. The RTL bunch held every advantage on the ground. If a full-scale assault by RTL was launched, it would be like a steamroller flattening an ant hill. Except they weren't ants, dammit, they were American fighting men. The best we have.

At that moment in time, Stratton couldn't help but wonder: what the hell makes us the way we are? What makes some men aggressors and others, defenders? Sure, everyone draws a pay check. But those risking the most on this night, those who were on God's side, they weren't mercenaries. An innocent woman and child needed to be rescued. Cody and Durell had come to undertake that suicidal mission. And they weren't backing down an inch no matter the odds, just like the men at that US base in Syria.

So where was Lieutenant-Colonel Willard Stratton?

Stratton's mood grew dark as the desert sky. He thought, *a pilot with my flight time, all my combat experience, and here I sit on the sideline twiddling my thumbs!*

He'd been raised in a military family, in a world where the male family history was nothing but military straight down through the generations; brought up to manhood the way some young men are raised to inherit the farm or the family business. Stratton's "business" had become service to his country.

His frustration was intolerable. He decided to do something about it. With a new energy burning in his gut, he stormed back into the headquarters building.

CHAPTER NINETEEN

At the base in Deir ez-Zour Province, Sara Durell had taken just about all of Captain Larson that she could stomach. The sidelong expressions she caught from Sergeant Samuels and some of the soldiers told her that she was not the only one.

She stepped from the command hut to find Larson and Sergeant Samuels still going at it. Nothing else had changed. Soldiers crouched along the perimeter, their collective attention centered on the activity of trucks and equipment that was now close to a half-mile away.

Sara had come to an abrupt decision regarding Larson a short while earlier, at which point she had excused herself while Larson was complaining to her and Samuels about the re-arranging they organized along the defense perimeter. Sara's time away had been only a matter of minutes.

As she rejoined them, she noted a couple have of things had changed between the company commander and his First Sergeant during her absence. For one, their dialogue had become edgy, more personal and not in a good way.

"Don't think I don't know what your game is, Sergeant," Larson was saying. "You and that CIA bitch are trying to undermine me, that's what you're doing. I ought to have you both thrown in the brig, you know that?"

There was a slur to his sneering words and a sense of inebriated imbalance in the way Larson kept shifting his weight from side to side.

"We don't have a brig, sir," Samuels said in a cool, reasonable voice. "We've got an emergency situation and we—"

"We've got a case of insubordination is what we've got," Larson snarled. "Samuels, I've got half a mind to—"

Sara made her presence known with a clearing of her throat. "From the way you're conducting yourself, Captain," she said, "I'm wondering if you've even got that much. Half a mind, I mean."

Larson whirled about to face her, almost losing his balance in the process.

"Bug off, you spy girl bitch. You're not in charge here."

Sara said, "That's what we need to talk about."

Larson waved her off, another gesture that nearly took him down. He returned his blurred vision to Sergeant Samuels.

"No more backtalk from you, boy."

Something dangerous was in Samuels' frown.

He said, "*Boy?*"

"You heard me. Order the men to open fire on those advancing on us. We're going to give these raghead bastards everything we've got. Pour it on!"

Samuels deferred to Sara. "Ma'am, those ain't our orders, are they? Our orders are to—"

Sara finished for him. "To not fire unless fired upon." Her eyes stayed locked on Larson like laser beams. "We don't have to like it but, yes, those are the orders."

Larson glared back at her. "I thought I told you to go away." His drunken anger powered each word. "Damn woman, you've got no place here."

Samuels chuckled a disparaging *tsk-tsk*.

"Now you've done it, sir. Something tells me the lady doesn't much like you and she's holding the ace card. She ain't one of us. She's straight out of DC. The Pentagon. That EA lets her call the shots. Am right, ma'am?"

"Right all the way, Sarge," said Sara. "Captain, would you know where I was these past few minutes?"

Larson snickered. "Answering a call of nature would be my guess. Damn split tail. Who gives a damn?"

"I did some work on my smart phone."

"Don't make me laugh," said Larson. "We're lucky to have communications at all out here in nowhere land. There sure as hell is no coverage for a damn smart phone."

Sara withdrew a slim black device from a pocket. She said, "My smart phone is really, *really* smart. With a satellite feed, it has a private hookup with the Oval Office."

Larson's drunken eyes stared blankly. "Oval Office?"

Samuels' said, "The White House, sir."

"I know where the goddamn Oval Office is," Larson rasped. "Are you bullshitting me?" he demanded of Sara.

She wagged the device before Larson's face. "Private issue," she said. "Comes with all sorts of bells and whistles and I was making use of nearly every one."

"I don't understand," said Larson.

He spoke in the plaintive voice of a child.

Sara said, "When I excused myself, Captain, I'd had it up to here with your unacceptable behavior."

"Unacceptable?"

"You're drunk, Captain. You're in no condition to command."

"I'm not drunk."

Samuels step forward. "He's been taking nips from a pint of vodka," he interjected, "whenever he thinks I'm not looking. Don't deny it, sir."

"Shut up, you," Larson snarled.

Sara said, "Captain, I took the liberty of recording a few minutes of your conversation with the sergeant before I excused myself."

"I didn't see you doing that," said Larson.

"You weren't supposed to," said Sara. "I transferred the file of the conversation to an email that I sent directly to the president."

"The president? What the—"

"I just received his reply. This is an official directive from your Commander-in-Chief."

Another chuckle from Samuels. "And they say the government takes too long to get things done. Dang, ma'am, you work fast."

Sara held up her really, really smart phone. A thumb flicked open the screen. She held the device out at arm's length in front of Larson's glassy gaze.

Larson weaved back and forth, trying to focus on the cell

phone.

"Hold it steady," he groused. "What does it say? What are you up to now, you bitch?"

"You've been relieved of duty," she informed him. "You are no longer in command here."

Samuels muttered, "Well, I'll be."

"You son of a bitch," snarled Larson. "You've been trying to undermine me all along! Wouldn't surprise me if the goddamn Syrians bought you off to take us all down. I'll fix you!"

He fought to maintain his balance, drunkenly pawing for the pistol at his side.

Samuels said in a conversational tone, "Sir, you leave us no choice."

Larson already had his pistol out. He said, "Huh?"

Samuels stepped in and delivered a sharp right to Larson's jaw. The drunken man's eyes rolled back in his head. He hit the ground like a felled tree, sprawling unconscious at their feet. Samuels blew on his knuckles.

He said, "Damn, that felt good. What next?"

"Have your men get the captain someplace out of the line of fire," said Sara. "And who is now the senior officer here?"

"That would be Lieutenant Perez."

"Have him report to me," said Sara. "He's your new commanding officer."

Samuels studied her with undisguised admiration. He said, "Ma'am, that is some powerful mojo you've got working for you, yes sir."

He started to turn away to follow her instructions.

That's when the roar of one of the RTL tanks boomed.

Seconds later the rear quarters of the HQ building exploded; a thunderclap of flame and a geyser of shrapnel and debris that showered everything.

Without hesitation, the US commandos on the perimeter of the outpost commenced returning fire, blazing through their ammunition with rifles hammering on full auto.

Sara and Samuels had both instinctively crouched to shield themselves from the shrapnel and debris as best they could. Rifle fire from outside the perimeter joined the steady firing from the base.

Sara caught Samuels' eye. She said, "Game on." She indicated to the unconscious figure of Captain Larson. "Let's get sleeping beauty somewhere out of the line of fire."

She grabbed Larson's ankles, Samuels got the shoulders. They carried him to under one of the oil company trucks that had been left behind. With that task done, Sara relieved the unconscious officer of the binoculars looped around his neck. She raised them to observe the battlefield.

The RTL mercenaries had left their vehicles, preparing to storm the outpost on foot. Flashes from RTL tank muzzles and machine guns lit up the night. The atmosphere shuddered with the cacophony of warfare.

Sara caught Samuels' eye as he was about to rejoin his men.

"Good luck, Sergeant." She gestured with her cell phone. "I'm putting through a call to 911."

CHAPTER TWENTY

Three stealthy, fleeting moon shadows approached the wall. Cody, Yavuz and Arjan advanced in fast zigzags, gaining the base of the wall, out of the line of vision of the sentries at the front gate. The sentries likewise were no longer in sight from this angle.

Yavuz hit a combat crouch, his back to the wall, his M4 and narrowed eyes watching in every direction. Arjan and Cody each slipped their rifle over the shoulder by its strap. Arjan knelt to one knee and cupped his gloved hands. Cody placed a boot into those clasped hands. Using his own body strength and leverage and the added boost of Arjan as a living stepping-stone, Cody gained the top of the wall. By reaching down, he was able to grasp Arjan's extended wrist, thus drawing the FSA man up to join him atop the wall. This procedure was then repeated, Arjan lying flat atop the wall, reaching down to assist Yavuz in joining them.

A simple drop of ten feet and they were in.

Three men. Three points of view. Three pairs of eyes piercing the gloom in separate directions in that first instant inside the walled oasis.

Yavuz spotted the danger first.

"Trouble," he whispered.

Cody whirled in time to see two Hezbollah sentries striding toward them from the rear of the compound; silhouettes in the tricky moonlight who reacted to this mutual sighting. Both fatigue-clad sentries fell away from each other, shouldering their AK-47s.

Arjan's right arm blurred. His combat knife flew from his fingers, whistling downrange to embed itself with quivering accuracy into the heart area of the sentry nearest them. The man emitted a gurgling death rattle and pitched off his feet in a spread-armed back-fall to land across the ground with a thud of finality.

The second Iranian soldier paid this no heed. He concentrated on unlimbering his AK in the flicker of time he thought he'd gained by his buddy's death, swinging his rifle into hurried target acquisition on Arjan.

Cody stepped out from behind Arjan and flung his knife.

Sentry number two caught the blade to the hilt through the throat, knocking him back off his feet, every bit as dead as the first one.

Yavuz joined Cody and Arjan. He patted the backpack he wore. "It is time for me to go to work?"

He was aglow with considerable enthusiasm. They had gone over Cody's plan during the briefing at the base.

"Go for it," said Cody. "Just spare one of the command cars and the tank."

Yavuz frowned his disappointment. "I do not get to blow up tank?"

"We may have use for it," said Cody. "Sometimes a tank comes in handy. Now get to it, demo man."

Yavuz gave them a thumbs up before he took off at a run, soon vanishing into the night.

The oasis slumbered, or seemed to. An errant breeze carried the smell of coffee.

Cody and Arjan moved along the wall in opposite direction of the front gate, deeper into the compound. Cody flattened himself against the back wall of one of the smaller barracks huts, beneath and to the right of one of the windows where a light had gone on. He motioned Arjan back.

Arjan heard the sound on his own. The two of them became indiscernible to the three Hezbollah troopers who strode past, AK-47s slung over their shoulders. Sleepy-eyed soldiers going on or coming off duty, jabbering away as if without a care in the world, moving past the spot where Cody and Arjan froze. The Iranians were heading in the direction of a tent across the way where lights were on and from where the smell of coffee originated.

When the three were out of earshot, Cody motioned Arjan to follow him and they silently hustled away from the barracks on a beeline for what Cody had determined to be where he hoped like hell they would find the hostages.

Then would come the real difficult part: getting out of here alive and in one piece.

* * * * *

Yavuz made it to his destination without hearing a sound or any indication or activity from across the oasis where Cody and Arjan would be. This met with his approval.

He advanced to one corner of a barracks, which shielded him from the center of the makeshift military base. From this corner, the next hut structure over could be seen, this one slightly different from the others as an AK-47 toting sentry stood posted at its front entrance.

Yavuz made a gentle purring sound of satisfaction to himself. He trusted Cody's assessment that the hostages were being held in the main building. That being true, the only other thing here worth a posted sentry would be where this Hezbollah detachment was storing its ammo.

A pair of Hezbollah officers emerged from the gloom, walking toward the ammo hut. The officers proceeded into the hut behind which Yavuz crouched under cover of shadows. The instant he heard their voices emanating from inside the hut, Yavuz broke from the corner to gain the back of the structure. Gaining the back of the munitions shed, he paused.

Kneeling at the base of the structure, he withdrew a wrapped square of C-4 plastic explosive from his backpack.

He wedged the HE against the base of the munitions building, inserting a detonator that could be triggered by a radio beep from a matchbox-sized device he wore clipped to his belt.

A couple meters beyond the munitions dump stood the vehicles: the armed Jeep-like vehicles and the two troop transport trucks.

Yes, the man Cody had lived up to his reputation, laying out a plan as they had before setting out tonight on this dangerous mission. Yes, it could work, locating the woman and her child—which Cody and Arjan were doing now—while he took care of wiring the munitions shed and these vehicles.

After the hostages had been whisked away undetected, pursuit would be out of the question. For Cody's plan to work, maximum silence had to be maintained. The whole plan depended on stealth and luck. Mostly the latter. Yavuz did not lie to himself about that fact.

He stood after having set the explosive. He left the building without the sentry in front ever having become aware of his presence. He hurried along the wall, advancing on the parked vehicles. After wiring them, he would stay to the wall and circle back around to rejoin Cody and Arjan before the building where everyone thought the hostages were being held. Then they would withdraw.

Yavuz approached the parked vehicles, moving first to one and then another, placing wads of C-4 and detonators against their petrol tanks, enough to take this motor pool out of commission.

The job was done.

He pulled away from the vehicles, moving toward the wall, the M4 held tight, its muzzle pointing the way. At first it seemed to him as if he would make it; that everything was falling into place, nothing could go wrong. He would unite with Cody and Arjan and continue undetected with no noise to alert the troops encamped here at this oasis. He gained the wall... and ran face-to-face with three Hezbollah regulars making a perimeter check along the inside of the wall.

The Iranians spotted him and reacted as one, falling away from each other, swinging their AK-47s around even as Yavuz tracked his own M4 carbine into target acquisition.

In that microsecond before all hell broke loose, before rifles from both sides opened fire, Yavuz knew there was no way *this* could be dealt with quietly.

* * * * *

Minutes earlier, Cody and Arjan had sprinted around the side of the main house and on into it.

A Hezbollah regular sat at a shortwave radio setup, not realizing he was in trouble until Arjan was already on him, death entering the house that fast. The soldier started to rise, going into a turn.

Scoping the layout in that first instant, Cody was already hustling toward a corridor that led off to the left.

Arjan looped a garrote around the radio man's throat from behind and pulled him back, with his knee into the small of the soldier's back. Arjan killed him like that, ruthlessly, efficiently, before the trooper had time to do more than reach both hands up in a grab for the strangling garrote that bit off his wind and ended his life.

Arjan stepped back, away, turning from the dead man before the body sank to the floor. Staying with Cody's plan, he tracked up his M4 and quickly returned to the outside where he crouched to cover their withdrawal track, holding a position beside the doorway with a clear field of fire.

Back in the corridor, Cody found an armed Hezbollah sentry standing in front of one of several closed doors, already in the process of bringing his AK-47 around and up when Cody came charging in at him. A quick slicing of the Ka Bar's blade severed the man's jugular. Cody utilized a quick kick to down the dead man, sparing spare himself from the sentry's geysering blood.

Cody tracked up his Glock, prepared for anything. The very presence of a sentry having been posted in front of this door made *this* the door. He delivered a powerful kick that sent the door inward, slamming against the inside wall of a room.

He stood in that doorway fanning the room with the Glock, then he lowered the pistol without firing. He saw no danger in here.

He saw only what he had come all this way to find.

CHAPTER TWENTY-ONE

Cody would remember the scene before him for the rest of his life: Mrs. Rashid, sitting up in bed with both feet on the floor, looking frazzled, wearing some sort of frock. She looked haggard but her eyes came to life in a hurry.

Between her and the door—between her and Cody—stood her 10-year-old son. The boy's feet were squarely planted. He held a broad blade knife fisted in his right hand. Prepared to defend his mother! A ferocious expression twisted his childish features.

Cody lowered the Glock. "It's okay, son," he said. "I'm here to take you and your mother home."

The tableau was broken by the sound of footfalls coming down a stairway that extended from the corridor.

Majid Baqir, awakened from his deep sleep, hadn't taken time to properly arm himself, but he came at Cody anyway like an attacking bear, charging down the steps with a lead-filled blackjack in his fist. He launched himself at Cody, who simply stepped aside. Cody took a swat at the guy's head with the Glock, hoping to brain him and keep this quiet, but his swipe missed and the terrorist crashed to the floor with an agonized groan.

Majid's swan dive distracted Cody long enough for Abdul Kemal to storm him from his blind side. Kemal grabbed Cody's wrist in the instant that the pistol was arcing around after having missed Majid. The Glock jarred from Cody's grasp and went clattering to the floor.

Cody responded with a left hook to Kemal's jaw, and then he smashed a knee between this terrorist's legs. Kemal gasped and started to double up. Cody drove a heel-of-the-palm blow under the Iranian's jaw. Kemal landed on his butt, dazed by the barrage of blows that would have put most men in dreamland.

Majid was starting to get up, drawing a pistol from the holster at his hip. Cody punched him in the mouth with his right fist. Majid staggered backward, but he still held the pistol. He shook his head and charged. Cody swung a snap kick to the guy's groin. The terrorist howled with pain, dropping his weapon.

A flash of movement warned Cody of further danger. He glimpsed the black leather shape rocketing toward his head in time to block it with a shoulder. The blackjack struck hard. Pain shot through Cody's left collarbone and his arm trembled in a muscle spasm. He pivoted to face his opponent.

Kemal had picked up the blackjack dropped by Majid, and lunged at Cody. It was apparent he knew some martial arts moves but he didn't know much about hand-to-hand. He charged without blocking, his right hand rising to deliver another blow with the blackjack.

Cody let him close in and abruptly slammed a right that broke the terrorist's nose, sending him back onto his butt. Cody reached down to retrieve the fallen Glock, but an unexpected blow between the shoulder blades canceled that motion, causing him to lose his balance. He started to fall but instinctively caught the floor with his hands, glancing back at the man who had hit him.

Majid was standing over him, preparing to deliver another kick.

Cody's boot lashed back first. He braced himself on his hands when he delivered the hard kick. Majid gasped painfully when the heel of Cody's boot caught him in the gut. He doubled up, coughing and choking. Cody sprung up from the floor and whipped a back fist stroke across Majid's face. Majid once again dropped to the floor.

Kemal wasn't out of action yet; broken nose, bloodied face and all, he was coming at Cody with the sap held high. Cody dodged the blow and Kemal's arm whirled past him. Cody slashed a karate chop at the nape of Kemal's neck. The terrorist fell on all fours. The guy was built tough, that was for sure. Without slowing, he made a speedy crawl toward where the Glock lay. Cody moved in and stomped the back of Kemal's head. He stomped it hard enough to crush Kemal's skull, sending blood spurting out both ears with the terrorist's dead face ground into the floor.

Cody spun about just in time to see Majid give up the fight.

Majid saw what had happened to Kemal and only wanted to blindly get away. He flung himself through the doorway of the room where the hostages were being held, telling himself he could find escape from another exit. But that's as far as he got.

Denise Rashid had left the bed. She and Ali stood just inside the room, shielded from sight of the action in the corridor but aware of every grunt, groan and body slam. Denise stood with her left hand reaching behind her to brace her little boy's back, shielding him. In her right hand she held the vicious-looking knife Ali relieved from Majid. She felt the revved-up tension, like dynamite about to explode.

When Majid came storming through the open doorway, she did not hesitate. Before the pig knew what was happening, she had shoved Ali back to safety before stepping into Majid's and sinking the knife's blade low into his gut.

A flash of release thrilled through Denise when Majid abruptly stopped his forward movement, the blade having sunk in to the hilt. She gave the blade several twists, remembering what this foul piece of shit had done to her.

She heard herself saying, "Here's your knife, asshole."

She pulled the blade out and rammed it in two more times, savoring his blubbering death rattle, the gore bubbling out from the sides of his mouth. He stared into her eyes with a final dawning awareness of what was happening to him. She released the knife handle and stepped away.

Majid collapsed, dead.

Denise started to feel tremors, uncontrollable, pulsing through her as she stared down at what she had done.

Ali moved quickly and efficiently. He stooped down over the fallen man, tugging the blade from the corpse, wiping it free of blood on the dead man's clothes.

Ali again hid the knife beneath his garment.

* * * * *

On the far side of the oasis, Yavuz was first to recover in the surprise confrontation with the trio of Hezbollah sentries. He flung himself to the ground and using his elbows to steady his aim, he triggered a short burst from the M4 in the split second before the guards could open fire on him. One guard dropped sideways, a trio of bullet holes punched in his chest.

The other two opened fire, but Yavuz had taken his dive so fast, their initial salvo sent whistling projectiles peppering the air well over his head. By the time the two soldiers were lowering their aim, Yavuz had already rolled behind the nearest hut, out of sight. Their bullets ricocheted off the ground where he had been but nothing more. He came to his feet in the abrupt silence that followed. He would let the others make their move first.

Yavuz overheard them whispering to each other, then the crunch of their bootfalls on the gravel, telling him the approximate position of each. They had split up and were circling the structure, approximately equidistant around either side of this hut.

Yavuz leaned around one corner, kneeling as low as he could to add to the surprise. He triggered a burst and the Iranian's face exploded.

Yavuz stood and started to turn, preparing to take on the other fellow, but seeing that sentry suddenly appear before him he realized, with a shock, that he'd been outflanked. The man fired and two bullets slammed into the forearm stock of Yavuz's carbine. The black stock burst apart, the impact ripping the weapon from Yavuz's grasp. He whirled and fell to one knee, unholstering his pistol in a single fluid movement. He raised the pistol.

The enemy trooper thought he had Yavuz. He had not expected Yavuz to spin around with another gun held ready. The Iranian failed to react swiftly enough before Yavuz blasted a round into the guy's chest.

Yavuz rose to continue on.

* ≈ * * *

When he heard the chattering of gunfire from across the oasis, Cody knew the mission had gone south. Or more precisely, it at shifted into high speed hit-and-get mode. Yavuz had run into trouble obviously. Everything had been moving smooth and fast and silent...until now.

Cody reclaimed his Glock from the floor, holding it as he stepped cautiously into the room with only a glance down at Majid's remains. A pool of blood was already beginning to form beneath the terrorist.

There had been no shot and there was no sign of a weapon. Denise Rashid had done him in with a knife. So where was the knife? Cody dismissed the concern from his mind; that was her business. She'd been through hell. Hell, she was *in* hell right now, slipping into the grip of traumatic stress, shivering as with a terrible fever.

She beseeched Cody in a desperate voice, quavering with anguish. "Please...*please* take us away from here...I can't take anymore—"

"Don't break now," he told her. "We're getting out of here. Stay close to me."

Without relinquishing his grip of the Glock in his right hand, Cody scooped up Ali without comment. The child's eyes were wide saucers. God only knew how he was taking this in. Cody could not remember ever having been that age.

With the boy shielded as best he could in a protective hug, Cody left the room, Denise Rashid staying as close as possible in his wake. When they passed Kemal's body in the corridor and the garroted Hezbollah trooper, the boy's eyes opened even wider.

His mother averted her gaze.

Cody lead them from the building, expecting to find Arjan waiting for them, covering the withdrawal track. There had been no gunfire except for what carried from the other side of the oasis.

Cody drew up short.

The command car sat there waiting, as expected, but a man stood between Cody and the vehicle. The man held an M4 carbine aimed directly at Cody.

He said in a cool, commanding voice, "You will stop where

you are. Drop your weapon. Pitch it this way."

This one was a sharper number than the three Cody had just eliminated. One of those had been a Hezbollah trooper, the other two terrorist thugs. But not this one. This one was well-groomed, his pressed suit making him look no less dangerous with the carbine in his steady grip.

Cody let the Glock go with an underhanded fling that dropped the gun near the Syrian's feet. Cody then set the little boy down.

Ali hurried to his mother's side, not hiding behind his mother, as Cody might have expected.

Cody's reasoning was that—with the Ka-Bar sheathed at his chest and a hidden pistol, not to mention and his bare hands—he wasn't wholly forfeiting his self-defense. But the man's command brooked no response save obedience. And there were the lives of Denise and Ali Rashid to think about. Cody hadn't come all this way to serve them up for slaughter.

He must keep this man talking. As long as they were talking, there was life; where there's life, there is hope. Cody would play any angle he could to buy time. There was still Arjan and Yavuz was hopefully out there on the loose in the night. Something would happen. Cody needed only to buy time for that something.

He said, "Who are you?"

"I am Fared al-Hor," said the man. "I am in command here."

Cody glanced about, indicating the inactivity around them. "Your military detachment is slow to respond."

Fared sneered along the length of the M4. "It will look better on my report to Damascus if I take you down single-handedly. And I shall." Fared nodded to indicate something off to their side. "Your companion was hardly up to the task assigned him," he added.

Cody's eyes had grown accustomed to the dark in the moments since leaving the lighted interior of the building. He could now see, without difficulty, the crumpled body of Arjan. He lay not far from the entrance in the illumination from inside, now clearly visible. The handle of his own knife had been plunged into his back.

Mrs. Rashid said in a small voice, "Oh, dear."

Fared snickered. He was enjoying himself, smug as could be. He said, "The fool was so busy preparing for your retreat he forgot to cover his own back. I strangled him and finished the job with his knife." He gestured with the M4. "And now I will kill you with the dead fool's rifle. It pleases me to make it all end for you in this way, American."

"Pretty damn impressive," said Cody with no sense of sarcasm, keeping the conversation and himself alive. He was thinking, *Where are you, Yavuz?* He said, "A man of your caliber would be in charge, ordering Hezbollah troops about. Go on, dude, you've earned bragging rights. The whole Rashid kidnaping is your deal?"

Cody's reading of the guy was right on. Anyone so well-tailored and well-groomed, so cool and collected as this fellow during an early AM firefight had to be prideful. In response to Cody's praise, the M4 never wavered but sure enough, the Syrian paused and his chest swelled with pride.

"Indeed this is my operation," he said. "Upon my return to Damascus, I shall be covered in glory due to its success. It did not take your country long to respond, I see."

"America takes care of its own," said Cody.

Fared smirked. "Ah, a patriot and hero to the end. Very touching. Have you any last words, American hero?"

Cody stepped forward a pace, confronting Fared, positioning himself between the Syrian and the two hostages. He said, "Spare Mrs. Rashid and the child. You've got me. There's no reason for them to die."

"How very gallant," said Fared with another snicker. "But you see, it was never the plan that they should survive." His expression hardened into that of a man about to pull the trigger. "Enough," he snarled. "No more talk. You have traveled all this way only to die with them, American pig."

CHAPTER TWENTY-TWO

So it ends like this! Cody thought. Well, hell. But then what the hell should he have expected?

This confrontation, this moment in time, was really what Cody's return, his "revival" comeback after the terrible loss of his family, had been all about right from the start.

Missions like this one.

Lately though, the path of Cody's life during those missions from which he did manage to return from, had brought him to a place where he had again found something worth living for.

He'd returned mission after mission feeling each time that he'd made the world a safer place. It had been a hell of a ride. And now, after all that suffering and healing and bloodshed, Sara Durell was in his life, waiting for him to return from this mission.

And there was this mission itself: Denise Rashid and Ali did not deserve to die like this. Cody had failed them. His last thought would be that bitter truth in his gut when the bullets blew him apart.

The series of explosions, coming from the direction of the motor pool on the other side of the oasis, smashed open the night like a slap across the face. Everyone's instinctual response was to jerk their gaze for an instant in the direction of the explosions that tore the night apart with saffron flash.

Everyone looked...except Cody. Two words flash across Cody's mind—*Thanks, Yavuz!*

He flung himself into action, hurling himself at Fared in the flicker of time during which his attention was distracted. Cody plowed into him like a football tackle with enough forceful momentum to send them both plunging to the ground, the rifle jarring loose from Fared's grasp.

Both men leapt to their feet. Fared had not been through the same degree of physical exertion this past hour as Cody and so he had the slightest edge in speed. He lashed a roundhouse kick to Cody's ribs. Cody groaned and staggered. Fared hooked the heel of his palm to the side of Cody's head. The blow knocked Cody to the ground. He rolled onto a shoulder and landed on one knee.

Fared raised a hand to deliver a sword hand chop. Cody jumped up from the ground and drove both fists into his opponent's torso. The double punch knocked Fared backward. Cody swung a high Tae Kwon Do kick at the Syrian's face. Fared's head whipped out of the path of the flashing foot.

Cody's balance was thrown off when his foot failed to connect. He pivoted awkwardly on one foot. Fared hooked a quick kick to Cody's back, hitting him above the left kidney. Fared slashed the side of his hand at the nape of Cody's neck. Cody turned and blocked that attack with a forearm, jabbing a fist to breastbone and followed with a left hook to the Syrian's jaw. Then Cody hit his opponent on the point of the chin with a karate punch.

Fared stumbled backward. Cody snap-kicked the Syrian in the midsection, the ball of his foot striking Fared hard in the stomach. Fared folded from the kick, but then managed to thrust both hands under Cody's ribs, rigid fingers stabbing like knives. Cody gasped, his breath driven from his lungs by the vicious double spear hand stroke. Fared butted his forehead into Cody's breastbone.

Cody staggered. Fared's hand streaked toward Cody's face, two arched fingers aimed at the eyes. Cody jerked his head aside. The Syrian stumbled forward and Cody hit him under the jaw with the heel of his right palm.

Fared fell backward. Cody grabbed his opponent's right wrist and twisted his arm, locking it at the elbow, his foot hooking Fared in the lower abdomen. The Syrian groaned and doubled up. Cody prepared to deliver another kick, but Fared suddenly dropped to the ground. He caught himself on his left palm and a knee as he lashed a sweeping kick at Cody's ankles. His leg chopped Cody's feet out from under him.

Cody landed on his back, still holding onto his opponent's arm. Fared rolled with Cody's movement and lashed a kick into Cody's gut. His left hand clawed at Cody's face. Cody clubbed the attacking fingers aside with his right forearm and punched the Syrian in the mouth.

Fared fell back but managed to swing another kick at Cody. Cody released Fared's arm and pumped both fists into his opponent's shin to block the kick. The terrorist boss quickly rolled away and rose to his feet. Cody got up just as fast this time and they squared off once more.

Cody feinted with his left hand and stomped a sidekick for Fared's kneecap. The Syrian moved his leg to avoid the kick, and slashed a clawed hand at Cody's right arm. Fared's other hand stabbed a hard spear hand thrust to Cody's sternum. The blow stunned Cody. He staggered away from Fared. The terrorist's right leg swooped into a crescent kick, smashing Cody in the side of the face. Cody fell to the ground. His head felt as if his skull had been split open. His chest was constricted, the lungs refusing to draw air.

Fared staggered toward his fallen opponent. His well-groomed appearance was a mess. He was breathing heavily, blood pouring from his crushed mouth. His expensive, pressed threads were dirty and torn. He uttered ugly animal sounds because the hinges of his jawbone had been dislocated by blows received during the battle. The American was good. Very good. But Fared felt he had won! He raised his stylish Italian shoe, now scuffed and ruined, to stomp this American pig's face into pulp.

Cody jerked his head aside. The heel of Fared's foot hit the ground near Cody's right ear. He thrust his left fist upward and drove a devastating punch between Fared's legs with all the force he could muster. Knuckles smashed into the terrorist's genitals. A testicle burst.

Fared howled in horrible agony, and doubled over. Cody's right hand shot, fingers stiff in a spear hand thrust. The tips of his fingers struck Fared in the center of the throat. The Syrian's windpipe collapsed and he fell backward, his hands clawing at his crushed throat as he twitched wildly on the ground. The terrorist boss kicked and thrashed in hopeless fury. Then his body sprawled in final defeat, and the last flicker of life vanished from him.

Cody propped himself up on an elbow and watched Fared die. His vision was blurred, and he felt as if he might pass out at any moment. But damn, at least he was able to breathe again. Dragging himself to a kneeling position, he reclaimed his Glock. He slowly attempted to rise. His head was clearing, his strength returning. He became aware of Mrs. Rashid and her standing before him.

Denise Rashid was leaning forward expressing unspoken concern with body language gestures and expression. Her boy, as always, stood close by her, silently observing. Not responding.

A new voice boomed, "Ah, there you are."

Yavuz sounded jaunty enough as he materialized from the shadows, his M4 held in a two-handed grip. He looked winded, with the battered look of guy who's just wrestled a bear. A testament to how damn fast this was all going down, thought Cody. No more than minutes had elapsed since their small team had come in over the wall. Sight of the reappearing FSA trooper was enough to reinvigorate him.

He said, "Good work, Yavuz. You cut that one mighty close."

"Ran into trouble."

"I heard. Glad you made it." Cody indicated Mrs. Rashid and the boy. "Let's get these two out of here."

Yavuz was looking around them. "Where is Arjan?"

Cody pointed, drawing the militiaman's attention to the curled up body. He said, "I just killed the man who killed him."

Yavuz's lined features remained stoic. "That is good to hear. Arjan has a good woman and three daughters at home. There will be many who will mourn him. He was a fine man."

"He died a damn good soldier," said Cody.

A sudden volley of rifle fire from across a clearing made all four of them duck for cover. The hail of bullets narrowly missed them, riddling the air and the command car, a Russian vehicle of indeterminate make and vintage; its windows were blown out in a million pieces, the vehicle riddled like Swiss cheese, the tires blown from their rims.

CHAPTER TWENTY-THREE

When there was a break in the incoming fire, Cody said, "The Hezbollah commander saw what happened to their man from Damascus. Now they want our blood. Yavuz, I'm getting Mrs. Rashid and Ali out of here. What was that you said about learning to work a tank back when you were in the Syrian Army?"

Yavuz grunted in the affirmative. He said, "You take hostages around back of building. Arjan was to cover extraction, no? I take his place. I get to tank. You get to side-by-sides. Okay?"

"Okay," said Cody. "Thank you, my brother. Give 'em hell."

Yavuz flashed a wide smile of bad and missing teeth. "Big fun," he said. "Always love tank! Kill many Hezbollah!"

Sporadic fire commenced from across the clearing. Angry flashes of saffron. Bullets whistled too close for comfort, shattering nearby glass and pinging off the metal. Ricochets screamed into the night.

Mrs. Rashid looked at Yavuz, deep emotion in her eyes. She said, "Thank you. May God bless you," barely audible say through the noise.

Yavuz did not know what to say. And so he said nothing. He turned, crouched and opened on the Hezbollah troops, returning their fire with a sustained burst from the M4.

Cody guided Denise and Ali in the opposite direction, quickly around a corner, taking them out of the line of fire. They hurried along, the woman and boy needing no encouragement to keep up with the brisk pace set by Cody. They gained the front gate, now unattended.

Hezbollah troops were infamously under-trained and gutless. With all the activity at the front of the building, the commanding officer apparently had ordered the front gate sentries to leave their post and join the fray. Either that or the sentries had decided to simply find cover and lay low until the fighting burned itself out. Such was the Iranian way.

They passed through the makeshift front gate that had been erected when the Hezbollah force first moved in. Once past the gate, Cody picked up their speed, breaking into a not-strenuous, loping run. Again the woman and boy had no difficulty in keeping up.

Dragged out as he felt, an inner drive was pushing Cody well past even his own endurance level. There was no feeling quite like a plan coming together and a mission hitting the right numbers before it went south and the killing started. So now there remained the not particularly long but extremely dangerous journey ahead to the small isolated US Army outpost in Syria.

Cody's gut was a tight knot of concern. He'd left Sara under siege, facing not only the advancing RTL force but also the dangerously incompetent Captain Larson. His concern was for Sara and for every man on that base. A dangerous trip, yeah, escorting his charges, this shell-shocked woman and her unreadable little boy.

Cody intended to let nothing, absolutely *nothing*, stand in their way.

Three stealthy, fleeting moon shadows withdrew from the oasis.

* * * * *

Yavuz continued trading fire with the soldiers for another minute after Cody's withdrawal. The Hezbollah troops firing on him were staying well behind cover so he was not scoring any hits among them. On the other hand, they were so dug in behind their cover there was little show of initiative in advancing on him.

Laying down a heavy fire along his backtrack, Yavuz withdrew, following the same path around the side of the building as had been taken by Cody and the hostages. The incoming fire from the troopers continued spraying filling the air with whistling projectiles when he did round the corner after hesitating only to fire a final, sustained burst in their general direction.

Then he ran toward the idling T-54 Russian tank. It's exhaust fumes hung in a bitter cloud that irritated his eyes.

A lone Hezbollah trooper had been posted to guard the tank. This one had apparently not received the memo concerning the

Iranian way. He raised his AK-47. Yavuz dropped to one knee before the soldier could trigger his rifle and triggered a burst from his M4. The guy's head recoiled violently. He went down, a mist of pink and gray spewing from his bullet-shattered forehead.

Yavuz reached the front of the tank. He crouched down. No one else seemed to be present. The hatch was open to circulate air. He climbed aboard, piling into the tank through the hatch over the driver's compartment.

In the fighting compartment of the turret, it took him only moments to re-familiarize himself with the controls. He checked the cannon shells in the ammunition storage bin. He didn't have much time. He should withdraw now that Cody and the hostages were gone. But he could not deny a strong temptation to shell everything in sight.

The T-54 was one of the best the Russians had. The tank had a 140mm gun. Its shell left the barrel at a velocity of 5000 ft. per second. The cannon itself was stabilized by means of delicate but armored equipment. Its big gun maintained an angle and bearing set by the gunner. The gunner rotated the turret and turret platform by means of pedals in front of his seat.

Yavuz was surprised at how comfortable and familiar it all felt when he slipped into the gunner's chair. Pushing down the cam-lever to his right, he pulled open the breech and shoved a 140mm armor-piercing shell into the chamber of the big gun. Then he closed the breech and locked the cam-lever. All that remained after that was the press of a button. The gun was ready to be fired electrically.

At this close range, he wouldn't have to do much aiming. With one hand on the wheel that elevated the gun and his feet on the turret-turn pedals, looking through the gunner's periscope that was synchronized with the range finder, he dropped the barrel and moved the turret until the pattern on the scope was right where he wanted it: dead center on the clot of Hezbollah troopers now holding their fire right there in front of the building. He was seeing them from a perfect angle.

He pushed the firing button. The gun roared. The AP shell hit with a ground-shaking roar, exploding bodies and body parts high into the air amid a tremendous fiery eruption.

In the confines of the overheated tank, Yavuz could not contain a shriek of unmitigated pleasure, witnessing the destruction he was delivering. He screamed, "Die, you scum-sucking sons of diseased whores!"

Then he sank back in the gunner's chair. Took a long and deep breath. Exhaled slowly, reminding himself to stay aware and collected. Thinking, *What have I become? I was an architect before the war. Cool of mind and manner. Now I cheer the death of others. I hate them for what they have turned me into. It is a pleasure to kill them. Let it be done!*

By now the American, Cody, had enough of a head start. What a man, that one! Yavuz had volunteered for this mission and had not regretted the opportunity to work with and learn from a trained operative like the American. The mission had been a success! Yet a sad time would come when Yavuz visited Arjan's home. How painful it would be to tell his wife that Arjan would not be coming home; that she was a widow. Nothing remained now but delivering this damaging news. Then he would withdraw. Yavuz looked forward to reuniting with Cody. Perhaps they would work together again.

Yavuz rotated the gunner's scope, loading and firing again; doing his best to blow the enemy apart. Looking through the scope with sweat rolling down his face, he centered in on the main building and pressed the firing button. The big gun roared a third time.

The building and those in it were vaporized, demolished in another ground shaking, angry red ball of fire. Huge chunks of ripped masonry and parts of bodies burnt black soared upward and came down over a wide radius.

Hezbollah soldiers were running back and forth in panic. Good, his work here was done. Time to go.

Yavuz climbed the short ladder fastened to the platform, pushing inward on the lever that opened the hatch over the commander's cupola on the side of the turret. The hatch popped open. Gingerly, he popped his head above the hatch rim and looked around.

In spite of the destruction, there were still a few soldiers running from one pile of wreckage to another.

Suddenly, two Hezbollah troopers appeared less than thirty feet away. Instinctively, Yavuz ducked down as one of the troopers lobbed a grenade. The grenade fell short, exploding against the side of the tank.

Bits of shrapnel rained down, a few chunks stinging Yavuz's cheek. Otherwise he was unhurt. He swung around his M4 and leaned over the side hatch rim. The soldiers had dropped to the ground right after the grenade was thrown. Now they were scrambling to their feet, both easy targets. Yavuz opened fire, downing both enemy soldiers in a withering hail of lead.

He crawled out of the hatch, easing down the rear of the turret to crawl hurriedly across the hot transmission and engine louvres. He crouched, preparing his drop to the ground. He would follow on foot following the track taken by Cody and there would be his side-by-side, waiting where he'd left it to speed him away.

Mission accomplished.

He would never know who fired the bullet that killed him. An unexpected blast of slugs blew apart his back, the impact knocking him from the tank.

When the darkness closed in on Yavuz, it was forever.

CHAPTER TWENTY-FOUR

Hell was pouring down on the little army outpost. The fighting was growing fiercer and more close-in with every passing second. The night shuddered and quaked with the violence of warfare.

The assault had begun in earnest with a mixture of tank fire, large artillery and mortar rounds incoming almost nonstop around and inside the compound. The explosions filled the air with dust and shrapnel, sending the American commandos scrambling for cover behind dirt berms from where they returned fire without hesitation utilizing anti-tank missiles and machine guns.

The artillery barrage was so intense, other commandos sought cover in the foxholes Sara and Sergeant Samuels had overseen. Covered in dirt and debris, these soldiers kept emerging to return fire at the column of tanks advancing under the heavy shelling.

The Marines, though pinned down by enemy artillery,

fought tirelessly, feeding ammunition to red-hot machine guns and manning the javelin missile launchers scattered along the berms. Other fighting men had made it to their trucks and were using a combination of thermal screens and joysticks to control and fire the heavy machine guns affixed on their roofs.

None of this had much effect on slowing the advancing column of armored vehicles. The mercenaries had begun to leave their vehicles and were storming the outpost on foot.

It was looking bad. Real bad.

And the worst part was that Sara's "really, really smart phone" she'd been bragging about—not to mention depending on—had gone belly up. No reception. No bars. Nada. Same with the outpost's online contact with Qatar. The fucking RTL barbarians were about to massacre them unless she could get through to call in some backup.

What the hell was wrong?

Sergeant Samuels had acquired a M4 carbine for her, which presently hung over her shoulder. With the roar of combat hammering her eardrums, she'd voiced the feeling to Samuels that she'd prefer to be on the front lines with the men, fighting off these bastards, but Samuels and the new CO had reasoned with her. Getting herself killed along with the boys, playing the Alamo bit and going out in a blaze of glory, should not be an option.

She needed to continue trying to contact the world outside. She *had* to get through. For every man on this base, she was the lifeline to the outside world of President Harwood and the fighter squadrons at the airbase in Qatar.

And so here she sat in one of the barracks, little more than a shed furnished with cots and bunks, working the really, really smart phone, not getting damn thing out of it and cursing a blue streak that likely had her poor sainted mother spinning in her grave.

She set the cell phone down when she heard men shouting in Russian just outside where she'd stationed herself to facilitate communication. The shed was well removed from the front line perimeter of the base, yet the shouting sounded like it was right outside her door.

Sara stood and swung around the M4 into firing position. She approached the open doorway, her finger on the trigger. She stepped outside where flashes from tank muzzles, anti-aircraft weapons and machine guns had turned the night into a psychedelic light show of death and destruction.

Without warning, automatic fire erupted from her left. Men were shouting Russian to each other behind the muzzle flashes.

The defense perimeter had been breached.

Sara returned fire with the M4. A shriek announced she had hit a target. Then she saw Samuels sprawled upon the ground nearby, firing at the enemy with his rifle. Someone else opened fire as well. Sara fired another three round burst at the enemy and quickly dodged to a new position.

Bullets chewed up the air where she had been only seconds earlier.

Samuels look over his shoulder and acknowledged her presence with a thumbs-up before again spraying the attackers with lead.

The outline of a man's head and shoulders appeared behind Samuels, about to ambush him. Sara fired another burst. The attacker's head snapped back and he dropped, dead.

Samuels caught what had just happened. "Good shooting, ma'am," he shouted over the sounds of battle.

Sara acknowledged this with a quick thumbs-up of her own. She saw something moving to their right flank and triggered her M4, slamming another opponent with a lethal dose of high velocity rounds.

The muzzle flash of another weapon responded to her fire. Bullets tore into earth near her position. She was thinking analytically: this little bunch of mercs who'd made it through and onto the base were about to stage a frontal assault on her and the sergeant's position.

Samuels aimed at them and blasted four or five more slugs into the fog of battle. Voices shrieked in Russian. Then the sarge pulled the pin from a grenade and lobbed the blaster into their position. The grenade exploded. Two bodies were hurled into the air by the blast. That seemed to take care of this band of mercs who had somehow managed to break through. Sara saw the remains of at least four slain opponents. This little bunch was DOA.

Around them, the battle continued to rage.

Samuels was on his feet. "Thank you kindly, ma'am. You saved my life. I owe you one."

"My pleasure, Sergeant."

"But, uh, excuse me for saying so, ma'am, but aren't you

supposed to be sitting off on your own somewhere trying to raise us air cover?"

Sara reached into the ammo bag she'd been provided and palmed a fresh magazine into the M4. "You mean sitting on my butt somewhere safe? That got old, Sarge. And I can't get through. I'd say the Russians are jamming everything we've got. Guess my smart phone wasn't so smart."

Someone opened fire on them from a new angle. The bullets ricocheted off the building behind them. Too close. Samuels pivoted. Fired a three round burst. No more incoming from that direction.

"Maybe your phone smartened up while you were busy saving my life. Sure is getting hot around here."

"I'll keep trying," Sara assured him.

She returned to the barracks shed. Samuels rejoined his men in combat. Sara reached for the cell phone.

Their chances for survival on this base tonight were on the cutting edge. So much going down tonight, and yet with all that, it was the fate of her man Cody that coursed beneath her every thought and like a strong current driving under smooth water.

Where was Cody at this moment? Had he survived the rescue operation in Iraq? When would she be seeing him again? His presence here sure as hell wouldn't be a hindrance.

But one of the rules set down by her man before this or just about any mission was that, considering Cody's penetration of enemy sites was usually part of his missions, he would carry no means by which possible captors could hack otherwise secure realms of intelligence such as a communication device of any sort.

Well and good, thought Sara, *except for times like this.*

Her concern for the man was too deeply ingrained within her to diminish. They'd worked together even before Cody's terrible personal loss that had cost him his family. In the recent past, he'd confided in a moment of intimacy that it was Sara's love for him that had helped heal him more than anything. She chose to believe him. They'd worked together in the field in the time since; in hostile environments, most recently Afghanistan. They'd even fought off a wipeout attempt by a sinister force within the US government. Had all of that sacrifice and healing come to *this*? Dying in a remote desert firefight? Would her last contact with the man she loved have been watching him ride off with those two FSA militiamen?

Sara was ready to die tonight if it came to that.

She would die fighting.

The thing that bugged her most would be dying without knowing what happened to Cody.

CHAPTER TWENTY-FIVE

The Pentagon

They were sleepy-eyed filing into the War Room on the second floor; Calhoun, the CIA Director. MacDonald, Secretary of State. Lansdale, Secretary of Defense and Freeman, the president's National Security Advisor. Their sleepy eyes snapped wide awake when Sara Durell's voice came patched through the phone speakers.

This was the main terminus of all military communications systems connecting Washington to every military and naval command in the world. Tiered areas, overlooking a highlighted conference table, hummed with muted, concentrated activity as military personnel were at desks, computer consoles and communications equipment. All consoles were fully manned, with all evaluators present.

Display maps on the wall, changing once every four minutes, reported a running tally on the disposition of American military forces worldwide. Another bank of monitors relayed data updates from the National Command Center, connected to the War Room by a short corridor.

The president sat at the head of the elite group. Before each at the large hexagonal table was a yellow pad, pencils, a tablet and a glass of ice water. As usual, Harwood's best friend and confidant, Chief of Staff Jim Corbett, sat to the president's right. The president toyed with an aluminum diet soda can, which he'd opened minutes before. He was tapping the can absently on the desk top.

Corbett had been with the man for so long, he could read his old friend like the proverbial book; every nuance, every side glance, every offhand remark muttered in frustration could speak volumes to one who knew the president as well as Jim Corbett did. The tapping of the soda can on the desk top? POTUS looked cool enough to make a TV appearance if necessary, but Corbett read the signs of a man working on the edge of a balled-up tension. Tiredness around President Harwood's eyes indicated the long hours everyone here had been keeping.

Every wide eye in the room was on the large scale flat screen map of western Syria that dominated the wall behind the phone speakers.

Sara did not mince words, her every word punctuated by explosions and the rattle of automatic weapons fire in the background. "It's bad, sir. We're under heavy fire. Vastly outnumbered. They're breaching our defenses."

The president said, "I hear you, Sara. Keep your head down. Help is on the way. The Russians have been jamming our communication. Don't know how they did it. Some new level. Our tech people are starting to shut them down."

"We need air cover bad, Mr. President."

"This will get done," said Harwood. "I promise. I'll see you and Cody when you get back to Washington."

"Yes, sir," said Sara. She did not sound convinced.

The brief lapse in the conversation was emphasized by another explosion, closer to the phone then the last.

The line went dead.

Harwood said to his cabinet, "You heard me. Let's make it happen. Any questions?"

"Not from me," said Calhoun. "It's a dead-end with the Kremlin." His pale complexion had acquired a red tinge of emotion. "Moscow categorically denies that they have anything whatsoever to do with RTL and with what's going on."

"Same with Damascus," said McDonald. His habitual scowl was well in place. "Nobody knows nothing. Syria won't even discuss the matter."

"It's got to be a power play on their part with Moscow standing by, keeping an interested eye on things," said Latisha Freeman. "They're waiting like everyone else to see what happens next. If we let them get away with this, RTL will seize oil and gas fields and protect them on behalf of the Syrian government. We have no choice. The time for caution is past."

"You know where I stand and always have," said Lansdale, his manner as brusque as ever. "Annihilate the bastards. All I need, sir, is your word."

"Then here's the word," said Harwood. "Annihilate."

"Yes, sir."

Lansdale was reaching for his cell phone as he left the War Room. He was soon followed by the others.

Corbett was left alone to study the white knuckles of his best friend's fists that were clenched on the table and the steely eyes focused on the map of Syria.

Corbett said, "Well played, Marty."

"Should have called it from the start," rasped Harwood. "It better not be too damn late."

"It wasn't an easy decision to make without a crystal ball."

"I didn't want to start World War III. I wonder if I just did."

"Stop it," Corbett advised. "You didn't start this. And this one goes deep because of who's involved, doesn't it?"

"I sometimes think, Jim," said the president, "that you know too much about your chief executive."

"I watched you listening to that woman's voice."

"Those people are deep in my heart," Harwood confessed. "Both of them. Cody and Sara. That woman brought Cody back from hell. And he's the best man we've ever had. This started out for them as a simple mission to bring back two hostages from enemy hands, to prevent an international incident, and here we are with the world blowing up in our face. And with all of that said you're damn right. I'm hoping like hell that my friends make it through this one alive...despite the odds."

CHAPTER TWENTY-SIX

The dozen or so planes constituting the force package were approaching from the Al Udeid Air Base in Qatar at different speeds over the desert. They would be arriving at the target area, what pilots called "working the kill box," in a precisely timed pattern.

A nearby AWACS Command plane was acting as traffic cop. Navy and Air Force EF-111s, packed with powerful jamming transmitters, had cleared the way, throwing a high tech shroud over enemy radar and antiaircraft missile systems by transmitting patterns of white noise. It caused radar screens to go blank, forcing the SAM crews to turn on their own battery radar. Then the F4-G Wild Weasels had sailed in with their high speed anti-radiation missiles (HARMs) that locked onto the SAM batteries, disabling the radar antennas with specially designed shrapnel.

Next came the fighter planes.

Lieutenant-Colonel Wil Stratton's fighter jet, with Jeff Jackson, the weapons system officer, seated directly behind him, and the pair of F-15s holding formation with them, were angling north. Each plane was loaded for bear: AGM-65 Maverick missiles, AIM-9 Sidewinder's, and a fully loaded M61 20 mm six- barrel chain gun.

Back at the base in Qatar, Stratton had pled his case to his superiors, cut a corner here, broke a rule or two there and possibly put his future military career on the line—none of which mattered given the relief and energy he felt knowing that, thank God, he was finally away from behind that damn routine desk and was instead part of an attack force about to do something about an enemy force.

It helped that Jeff Jackson was not only a good friend but his record showed him to be the best WSO at Al Udeid. A fighter pilot's life depends on the man behind him. The WSO's responsibilities include keeping an eye on the radar screen, deploying countermeasures when taking fire, and more often than not activating the weapons system while the pilot maneuvers through unfriendly skies.

Stratton glanced at the video image of the upcoming terrain projected onto his heads-up display, mounted over the instrument panel directly in front of his line of sight. The HUD screen presented the pilot with all necessary flight and weapons information, while identical information was simultaneously presented on one of the WSO's CRT displays.

When they were two miles from the target area, Major Humphreys' voice crackled across the radio. "This is Falcon Leader. Falcon One and Two, flare out. I'm going to give these yahoos their wakeup call."

"Roger," Stratton said, and was echoed by the pilot of the third fighter plane. Taking orders from a junior officer was one of the minor concessions Stratton had made to gain the privilege of flying this mission.

With the throbbing hum of the fighter plane surrounding him, the terrain passing below him in a blur, he acquired visual sighting of the target: the array of tanks, troop carriers and assorted artillery; the swarm of mercenaries rushing about, besieging the army base adjacent to the oil company plant. The little outpost was making its last stand, fighting for its life. That was apparent even from a distance.

Stratton banked away in one direction while Falcon One flared off in the other, establishing a defense perimeter while Humphrey went in for the first strafing run.

There wasn't much chance of encountering enemy aircraft. Since almost the beginning of the war, the skimpy Syrian Air Force had remained largely inactive. And even if the Russians did manage to scramble a handful of fighter planes, the jammers would have already cut them off from their ground based command and control centers which is why the Russian jets were staying grounded or flying blind.

Antiaircraft artillery flashed like strobe lights as Falcon Leader made his run, dropping a one-thousand-pound bomb that mushroomed into a red fireball, blistering the sky brighter than daylight. Humphreys' plane banked away like a silver bullet.

"Take it, Falcon Two." The major's stern voice crackled

across the radio. "Good luck, men. It's mighty hot down there."

"Copy that, Major. Going in."

Stratton swooped around for the approach and started a steep descent, diving sharply at one thousand knots. He hit the afterburners and hurtled straight toward the target.

A sudden tone from the radar system indicated that a missile had been launched at them. Stratton maintained his course and speed, cursing under his breath. The HUD indicated the missile type as infrared-guided. It was less than a quarter mile away.

"Got it?" he snapped.

"Got it," Jackson replied.

Stratton executed a sharp evasive maneuver. He could feel his facial muscles fluttering under gravitational pull. He was thinking: *Damn! I'm lovin' this shit! Feels so damn alive to be back in action again!*

Jackson activated a flare, its blossoming burst of heat designed to draw the heat seeking surface-to-air missile off target. The concussion of the flare detonating came at the same time that the missile disappeared off the HUD screen.

The flare had done its job.

Stratton looped around for another approach. Flak was hammering the sky all around his jet.

This was always the trickiest part of a strafing run. Once a plane was directly over the site, it was relatively safe since the SAM launchers couldn't shoot straight up. The principal threat was the heavy antiaircraft fire they were being exposed to. In the next few heartbeats it could go by the numbers...or turn to shit. Wrapped in the keening sensation of high-speed aerial combat, Stratton retained a complete professional cool.

"Fire when you've got a lock on them, Jeff. This is one hell of a high threat area," he told his WSO.

"Target acquisition," Jackson replied. "Lock on."

The WSO targeted the item on the CRT image by placing the cursor on it, and the info instantly processed and down-loaded into the weapons system.

With a *whoosh* one of the Mavericks punched out, sizzling like a fiery finger, trailing smoke toward the source of the artillery flashes a half-mile away. The missile was a fire-and-forget variety and as soon as it was launched, Stratton maneuvered his plane into another break turn and resumed his holding pattern on the perimeter for Falcon Three to make its run.

After this softening up procedure would come the bombers.

Then it happened. They were climbing, flak exploding in angry flashes all around, when the plane was jolted mightily. Immediately the power of the climb slackened. The HUD started beeping and blinking: *Caution...Turbine failure...caution... turbine failure...*

Jackson cursed.

Stratton snapped, "Leader, this is Falcon Two. I'm hit. I'm dropping fuel."

Humphreys' voice responded instantly.

"Get the hell out of here now, Colonel. *Move it!*"

"Affirmative," Stratton replied. "Heading out. Okay, Jeff. Let's nurse this wounded bird home."

Jackson was already setting the cursor on his CRT for the

return flight.

Stratton hit the burners for a fast escape. The plane was a hell of a lot harder to handle at high speed when damaged, but all he had on his mind now was getting them back to Qatar. He hit the burners…and nothing happened.

The jet began to wobble precariously, then the nose dipped.

The hit they'd taken was obviously worse than he'd first thought. At this low altitude, chances were that they would go into an uncontrollable dive. When that happened, they would impact in seconds. Even now the aircraft was hurtling well off course, heading deeper into Syria.

"We're not going to make it, Jeff."

"I hear that," Jackson responded calmly. "Bail?"

"Bail," Stratton confirmed.

Simultaneously, they activated their ejection seats.

Stratton's body was violently expelled from the cockpit into the air. His body arced away from the jet that was already streaking groundward. He seemed to hang suspended there, high above the ground, the world a topsy-turvy panorama of endless, tumbling sky and earth.

Then there was only the sensation of falling, falling, falling…until the chute finally opened with a loud popping *snap!* Stratton's body jarred as his descent was checked. As he drifted downward, he spotted Jackson riding down not more than a dozen yards off to his right. They descended, the air so quiet that Stratton could hear his own labored breathing.

Their plane hit the ground. Stratton saw the flash and a moment later heard the explosion from two miles or more downrange. Jackson's eyes locked on the burning wreckage in the distance.

"Well, there goes twenty million of the taxpayers' dollars," he called over to Stratton.

The moon had set. The endless panorama of the earth, coming up to meet them, was like a black void opening to consume. Something caught Stratton's attention: the clustered lights of a small village of modest wood and stone dwellings. From that direction, along a road running close to where they would be touching down, and open for will drive vehicle, headlights on, was speeding in their direction.

"Forget the plane," Stratton called over to Jackson. "We've got company."

The vehicle left the road, bouncing across a flat, open field, continuing toward them.

Jackson saw it, too.

"Those bastards aren't going to take me alive, sir."

Across the distance and the muted sigh of air, Stratton clearly heard the gravelly voice of his WSO conveying resolve.

Stratton called back, "Jeff, don't do anything nuts. They could be locals just coming to see the excitement."

The optimism sounded hollow even to Stratton's ears. He and Jackson worked their risers, attempting to steer away from the road.

CHAPTER TWENTY-SEVEN

For the first time in his life, Dimitri Volkov, in the heat of a raging battle, felt totally and completely helpless. He didn't like the feeling. Throughout his life, even before signing on with RTL, Dimitri had always felt in control. Even at his lowest ebb in prison, he always felt there was a way he could make things better for himself.

But not this time.

Since having joined RTL, there had been no way he could feel helpless. Heavily armed. Surrounded by like-minded, hard and brutal men without morals. And a power behind them that without doubt had political connections in places as high as the Kremlin. As a soldier in RTL, one did not know fear. In Africa, in the Ukraine even enemy soldiers fled in fear because *he* was the one who was feared.

But tonight, here in the Syrian desert, with jets flying low overhead, strafing the RTL force with missiles, bombs and machine-gun fire, with the men he'd served with dropping left and right, some with their heads blown off, geysering blood, others with their guts hanging out...there was nowhere to turn. And there was the threat laid down at that prison recruitment. Crew chiefs in tonight's action followed and watched through the fog of war, prepared to gun down any RTL man shirking his duty.

When the first jet flew over, strafing, Dimitri had flung himself beneath one of the troop carriers. He'd managed to survive while those around him were mowed down.

After the jets came the bombers.

For the briefest, short window of time it had looked like they could take possession of this base as they'd been ordered to. Splinters of the attack force had managed to breach the defense perimeter despite heavy fire from the defending Marines. These were the toughest, meanest, deadliest American fighting men. The US Marines were famous throughout the world. It was only through overwhelming odds that RTL had expected to prevail tonight. But their resistance was almost inhuman.

And now that the planes were dropping their bombs. Men around Dimitri were dying violently by the hundreds, leaving him helpless, carried along on the human wave pushing him forward—a frantic wave now, not aggressive—men not attacking but fleeing for their lives, dispersing in panic from the thunderous, deafening carpet bombing.

Dimitri had come to hate the RTL. He should have served out his time in prison instead of signing up. Another year and he would have been released anyway. His sentence served. His debt to society paid. Free to walk the streets. Free to love the ladies and come up with ways to make money and survive.

Would he survive what was happening to him now? He thought he'd been so lucky to elude death earlier at the hands of the mysterious intruder. The fellow had gone on to kill General Pornov and Mahmoud after leaving Dimitri with only a clip on the back of the head. Lucky, yes. And now had his luck had run out? Had he survived that encounter only to be served up now as a human sacrifice to the dogs of war?

The fleeing, mindless, directionless group carrying him along somehow made its way inside the perimeter of the Army base. With the bombing louder than ever, seeming to eat up the earth and spit it skyward, the mercs as one started to realize their predicament caused by their mad haste to outdistance the bombs. That collective realization came even as US Marines spotted them and opened fire.

Their auto fire began toppling men around Dimitri, bullets shredding and rupturing human flesh, splattering the night with blood and body fluids. Mercenaries fell left and right before they could even fire a shot.

Dimitri flattened himself to the ground, surprised that he had not been hit. The sustained weapons fire continued to drop others while he scrambled madly across the ground like a crab. Holding onto his assault rifle, he managed to reach the corner of a building. He scampered around the corner, gaining cover with a quick glance over his shoulder that told him he was the only survivor of the group that had mindlessly stumbled its way onto the base in the panicky confusion of night fighting.

Dimitri lay there upon the ground for what seemed like the

longest time. In reality surely less than a minute went by before
it occurred to him that he must not remain there forever and
hope to live. He must shoot his way out.

Everything was now in chaos. The RTL crew chiefs were
lost in the fog of battle like everyone else. Dimitri assured himself that he would get away from this. He would live another
day. And he would not live in Russia! He would never again
touch a gun once he killed his way out of this mess.

He forced himself to his feet, gripping the AK-47 with his
right index finger curled around the trigger. The world around
him was bombs going off, bombers thundering by flying overhead, close-in fighting on the ground. He must withdraw.

He made it to the far corner of the building and peered
around its side.

That's when he saw her.

A woman, so out of place amid this carnage. And yet she
seemed to belong, to fit right in the way she stood there, standing apart from the fighting, a rifle slung across her shoulder.
She held a cell phone to her ear, facing in the opposite direction.
She did not see Dimitri.

Dimitri paused.

There in the crazy flaming darkness it would be a perfect
shot. He couldn't miss. Shooting a woman? She was the enemy,
after all. There had been incidents in Africa and the Ukraine
when he had been ordered to execute women. The only thing
that mattered now was killing as many of the enemy as he could
so they wouldn't interfere with his withdrawal.

He raised the assault rifle. Her back was squarely in his

sight. She was just starting to turn as he was leaning into the trigger pull.

Then, for Dimitri Volkov, everything ended.

Sara had pocketed the cell phone and was unslinging her M4 from her shoulder when the rifle shot to her left caused her to tense up and send a look in that direction. A mercenary, who had somehow managed to breach the perimeter, was slumping to the ground, the back of his head blown away.

Sergeant Samuels advanced from beyond the fallen man, a thin wisp of gunsmoke curling from the muzzle of his carbine.

Sara expressed her relief with a sigh. "You just saved my life, didn't you, Sarge? You don't waste time settling your debts, do you?"

Samuels gave one of his good natured chuckles. "Everything happens so fast these days," he said. "That's what they tell me on the internet." He dismissed the matter with a look skyward at a B-52 bomber thundering by low overhead after having dropped its load. He added, "Tide seems to be turning."

They had to raise their voices to be heard above the raucous racket enveloping them. Sara's eyes went to the fallen bodies near the perimeter. "Looks that way, doesn't it? I was trying to get through with a well done to Lieutenant-Colonel Stratton. But I only got his voicemail."

"Back to the salt mines," said Samuels. He took off at run toward the shooting sound of a skirmish nearby.

Sara watched him go with a sense of pride not only for the top sarge but for every man on this base. It did indeed look like the tide of this battle was turning. That began with the American warplanes arriving in waves: fighter jets, B-52 bombers and AC-130 gunships had pummeled the enemy troops, tanks and vehicles. The US soldiers had worked the radios to direct the bombers in.

At one point Sara was surprised to see a soldier exposed to incoming fire, using a missile guidance computer on his lap and NVD binoculars to pinpoint target locations and pass them on to the commandos calling in the airstrike.

Captain Larson!

Sara hurried after Samuels to continue the fight.

CHAPTER TWENTY-EIGHT

The return route from the Pentagon varied every time the trip was made and involved the rotation of a half dozen well-chosen and secured routes. Moving POTUS always required a security package minimum of six black window vans and SUVs to sandwich the limo as the motorcade traveled.

The president was glumly eyeing the street scene sailing past outside the limo's tinted windows. "So much for rehearsing our press conference," he grumbled.

They had canceled one scheduled media event where President Harwood was to have addressed a national convention of high school honor students. They'd also canceled the pre-press conference prep. But there were some events that could not be canceled, high among those was a White House press conference.

Usually these were handled by West Wing functionaries, the press secretary or one of her stand-ins, but lately the Harwood administration had taken a beating on several fronts, the economy and the upcoming midterm elections among them. The American people wanted their president to weigh in. The press conference had been arranged to appease and inform the electorate and was much anticipated. There was no escaping it.

Corbett sat next to Harwood, the only other passenger traveling in the chauffeured limousine. He said, "At least you're going in with the RTL mess off your back."

"True enough." The president nodded. "Too bad I can't tell anyone about it. An air strike taking out a couple hundred Russian mercenaries who were trying to kill American Marines would make me a hero."

Corbett sent him a cynical look. "Maybe for a week or so. Ten days tops. Then something new would come along and put us right back in the muck. Global detente is what matters here. Thought you'd learned politics by now, Mr. President."

"Ha ha," said Harwood. "Oh, we'll play the game, Jim. You know I have the touch. This second term wasn't handed to me on a platter."

"You have lost valuable prep time over this Syrian business," Corbett conceded. "When the cameras start rolling and the questions start flying, leaving Syria out of it has the added advantage of keeping it simple."

"We stand strong in all the policy areas we're being criticized for," said the president, "the economy and so on. But damn, Jim. Here we sit after what just went down, kicking some serious bad guy ass. Our fighting men displaying the determination and grit that makes America the world power the rest of the world depends on. But we can't crow about it."

"It's more than that and you know it," said Corbett. "I know you, Martin. You understand global diplomacy. You've got a personal stake in this with Cody and Durell."

"Damn straight," Harwood acknowledged with a grunt.

"But there's the practical matter of the Russians," said Corbett. "So far they're still maintaining their complete innocence in this affair."

"Innocence," Harwood snorted. "They should brag about getting their ass kicked?"

"No, but if Russia doesn't go public with what happened in Syria, *we* know it was the Kremlin okaying everything if not pulling the strings. The rest of the world will see through their bullshit, too." Corbett leaned forward to make his point. "But they have and will present a solid case for RTL being behind the attack and maybe they'll even administer a slap on the wrist to Syria for provoking RTL. But from our perspective, we keep mum. Victory in this incident yeah, it'll have to be enough."

"I get it," said Harwood. "If the Russians stay quiet about it, why provoke them. There's no way we're going to keep this out of the news forever. It's going into the record and the press has access there one way or another. But let's not make it easy for them."

Corbett grinned.

"You do get it. If the Kremlin doesn't make a big deal over what happened, we'll be smart to do the same. That could with pay off with a dividend the next time a crisis with the Kremlin pops up as it surely will."

"So we've avoided a world war by winning the battle," said

the president. "Yeah, it'll come out some day, everything does. But okay, we'll sit on it for now."

"I honestly believe it's for the best."

"But you do know that's not the only thing weighing on my mind, right?"

Corbett nodded. "Cody and Durell."

"Cody and Durell," the president repeated. "Those two sure got themselves caught up in something beyond a cut and dried hostage rescue mission, didn't they?"

"I'd call that an understatement," said Corbett. "At least we know Durell is making it through."

"That's one helluva woman," said Harwood. "A base under attack, loaded with Marines, and she steps in and takes care of business like a damn field commander."

"Mighty impressive," agreed Corbett. "We should be hearing from Cody soon enough."

"Unless something went wrong," countered Harwood, "and God knows there's enough potential for that. Okay, okay. We'll get this press conference over and done with and maybe I'll even get a good night's sleep tonight. You're right, Jim. Syria is off my back more or less. But my mind won't rest easy until I know where Cody is and what the hell's going on over there."

POTUS relapsed into his silence.

Not as glum as before, Corbett noticed.

Corbett let it be. At first when Cody returned and began this new phase everyone was calling Cody's War, the Chief of Staff had voiced his discomfort about the setup. He'd felt they were taking advantage of a not fully recovered man. In Corbett's mind it was much too much like the suicide by cop gambit. But he went with the flow on the matter and as the recent past missions of Suicide Cody tallied up, Corbett thinking on the subject changed profoundly.

Jack Cody was one of the best secret assets America had on tap.

James Corbett shared the president's concern for the man.

* * * * *

Ahmed Rashid was dreaming in a Rome hotel suite where he remained under the care of his American "handlers."

In the dream, it was years ago. He and Denise were on their honeymoon in France, a country that had seemed in the first heady days of their romance, to have been made for love. A most exclusive resort surrounded by woodland; hiking paths, sunshine, bountiful birdsong serenading them. A secluded stream running through the glorious, natural landscape. In the middle of that stream was a large, flat, sunbaked rock.

It was on that rock, with the stream burbling about them, before the eyes of God and no one else, where their beautiful lovemaking transpired. A never to be forgotten memory that lived again in Ahmed's dream. In the dream they were still making love when he awoke.

To his immense shock and surprise, he had a raging erection.

When the present flooded his mind, he broke out in a cold sweat. The erection diminished to the flaccid appendage that had not known eroticism since he and his wife and son had boarded that private, late night flight in Damascus; the first step in his defection, their "escape," to Rome.

Rashid sat up in the bed. He swung his feet to the floor and concentrated on his breathing. Within a minute or so, his breathing normalized and he was able to think clearly.

He thought about Denise. Their passion had never cooled with the passing of more than a decade of married life. They'd found a place of their own in the world. Not just the gated community in Damascus but in life itself. Denise wrote poetry though never published. Ahmed painted though his work was never shown. He'd long thought one only found that one true love in song, poetry and romantic movies. When he was with Denise, he knew such a thing was possible elsewhere. Then along came the blessing of Ali, the decent, sensitive, beautiful child that enriched their lives tenfold. He and Denise had found a world Ahmed hoped would never change.

It was Denise's grace and spiritual wisdom that had led him to a point where he could no longer tolerate what he'd allowed his life to become: a functionary in the corrupt, ungodly Syrian bureaucracy. And so he'd defected from his homeland with documentation of Syria's despicable war crimes, hoping in so doing to curtail them. This was Denise's gift to him along with Ali. And now that beloved family was in harm's way while he rested in these exclusive surroundings.

It was an intolerable situation.

He must do something.

How is a man's life judged by God or by his fellow man?

What does man leave in his wake after he's gone? Children. A career. The memories of those who knew him. The way he lived and the way he died.

The two human beings he loved the most were in mortal danger, might already be dead, because of choices he, Ahmed Rashid, had made. Actions he'd taken and nothing else was responsible. He knew what he must do. He must end this thing, this horror he had brought on his beloved family. There was no other solution. Hiding—luxuriating—in well-appointed accommodations while his world fell apart was a coward's way.

He *must* return to Syria.

His heart started thumping harder against his ribs with this epiphany; this decision. He hurriedly dressed and gathered what personal effects he could carry about his person. He was serving himself up to fate. He would travel light. He left the bedroom...only to encounter his CIA watchdog, Summers.

Their earlier conversation, when Rashid had submitted to Summers' urging to stay and not return to Syria, was etched clearly in Rashid's mind. He told himself that would not happen this time. He became aware of his heart pounding in his chest.

Keep going, he told himself. *This time, nothing will stop me!*

Summers had been sitting on a couch, referring to his cell phone. He promptly rose to his feet, seeming to naturally position himself between Rashid and the front door. Usually a second agent was about but there was no sign of him at the moment.

Good, thought Rashid, heart pounding faster than ever.

Summers was obviously trying to downplay his intense

demeanor. He spoke in a friendly, conversational voice. "Whoa there, Mr. Rashid. What's the rush? Where are we off to?"

"You must know where I am going," said Rashid. "You're a man. I am off to do what I can to save my wife and child. Please, Mr. Summers, do not try to stop me."

Some of Summers' intensity surfaced but he remained cool.

He said, "Well now, I thought we'd hashed that out, Mr. Rashid. We had an agreement, remember? A few hours ago you granted us six hours to bring your family home. I told you we're on it."

"And what have you heard from this Cody, the man you have such faith in?"

"We're waiting to hear. Be reasonable. Please, Mr. Rashid."

"I am a man," said Rashid. "I am finished being a passive observer. No more. My woman and son need me. Kindly step aside."

Rashid's heart was beating so fast now, it sounded like thunder in his ears. He could barely hear his own voice.

Summers did not budge. He said, "Do you think you're the only one with skin in this game? I've got three agents lying in the morgue downtown, murdered by these bastards yesterday morning. Those were my people, do you understand that? Their souls are crying out to me for vengeance. I hear them even when other people are talking to me. You think I don't want to be out there on the street chasing down those responsible? I do, Mr. Rashid. Believe me, I do. But that's not my job. My job is you."

"While another man—your man, Cody—risks his life," said

Rashid. He was feeling no contempt for Summers; rather, he was sympathetic to the man's position. But he was not about to back down. Summoning as much strength as he could summon, he said, "Your Mr. Cody could at this moment be lying dead in the desert. No, Agent Summers, I will remain inactive any longer. I want to know my wife and child are safe. I will not find that out by remaining here doing nothing. Now kindly step aside."

Rashid had no wish to speak further. He'd said all he needed to say, he reminded himself. He must think clearly. Why was doing so suddenly becoming difficult? He must continue on in haste, without further hesitation. Had they dimmed the lighting? He found himself growing weaker with each passing second.

Summers appeared disinclined to step aside.

Rashid started around him when he suddenly realized he had lost the ability to breathe. The room started to spin around him. His final awareness was of Summers reacting with alarm, turning and reaching out for him with both arms. Rashid experienced the strange sensation of falling into a bottomless black pool.

And then nothing.

Summers caught the man before Rashid hit the floor. He eased the unmoving fellow upon the floor lengthwise.

Agent Billings stepped in from an adjoining room. He observed Summers kneeling on one knee beside Rashid. He said, "Trouble?"

"Not for Mr. Rashid," said Summers.

Billings was a right new man with the agency, not always attuned to nuance. "Should I call the doc?"

They had a 24-hour physician on standby.

Summers said, "Wouldn't do him any good."

The dead man's eyes were wide open, staring at the ceiling. Summers used a gentle thumb to close the eyelids. *Too damn bad*, Summers thought. Rotten way to check out. More pressure than the poor guy could handle brought on a heart attack that took him out.

Thing was, Summers could appreciate and share Ahmed Rashid's frustration, sitting on the sidelines, stressed because there wasn't a damn thing you could do when so much was at stake.

But there was one concern Summers shared with the dead man.

What had happened to Jack Cody?

CHAPTER TWENTY-NINE

Iraq

Cody was making a run for the Syrian border, pushing the side-by-side to its limit. Denise Rashid sat in the passenger seat beside him, with Ali asleep in her lap. Her son's head rested against her chest, the top of his curls nestled under her chin. Her arms securely cradled the boy.

Cody figured there was no way he could get them across the uncharted wasteland the way he'd approached the oasis. Making it home to the American base in Syria without the guidance of the FSA men who'd brought him to the oasis was putting Mrs. Rashid and the boy in more danger than was necessary. He simply didn't know this country well enough. And so he chose to risk traveling along the highway, which was really nothing more than a two lane, straight as a ruler blacktop in serious need of maintenance that ran past the oasis.

The first hint of a false dawn was limning the horizon with

a thin strip of pale gray. The world for now, though, remained a dark place, the road littered with felled power lines and shell craters. Cody didn't turn on his lights, relying on the vehicle's mounted thermal imaging camera to navigate.

It was a rough ride.

Under less unsettled circumstances, Sara could have drawn on the military resources at hand to locate Cody and the rescued hostages. He knew for a fact that there were US satellites capable of reading a license plate down here on earth from their orbit in outer space and Sara knew the location of the oasis.

But these were distinctly *un*settled circumstances.

Like everyone else in the 21st century, Cody had largely come to rely and to appreciate and use technology. He did choose, however, not to rely solely on it. His faith in its efficacy was not absolute.

He wanted to get back ASAP to the base in Deir ez-Zour. When he'd left, they'd been preparing for an imminent attack by the RTL force. His return could unfortunately place Denise and her boy in danger again. But that could not be avoided given these unsettled circumstances. If the fighting still raged when they arrived, he could only do his best to protect them, but he had to make a difference, if he could, to assist Sara and those soldiers, fighting for their lives, that he'd been forced to leave behind when he and the FSA men headed out.

Denise kissed the top of her little sleeping boy's head. She said in an audible but spaced-out voice, "How nice it would be if this little one could wake up and find that he'd only been in some terrible dream; that he was back in the beautiful, safe world he knew."

"That would be nice for all of us," Cody agreed.

Denise had lost track of time. At first, after the awful massacre in Rome and her and Ali being whisked away, she'd gone into shock. It seemed like she was watching a movie, registering everything that happened with clarity and yet watching it happen to someone else. Then, once they reached that oasis where the Hezbollah troops were waiting, it had been almost a calming breather from the slaughter then the flight by air. At the oasis she'd been able to rejuvenate. The attack from Majid had actually served to sharpen her senses which led to her and Ali making their escape attempt. After that incident, she had felt restored, bonding with Ali. But now all of that was gone. Evaporated. She now felt only a numbness pervading her senses.

And it was no particular blessing that, as they sped along in the side-by-side, her mind continued to think.

She said, "Why does it always come to violence with men?"

"Not always," said Cody.

She went on as if she hadn't heard him. Maybe she hadn't, what with the road sounds of the side-by-side racing down the highway. On the other hand, he could hear her just fine.

She said, "It's always been that way throughout history. Men ruining the world of decent people by propagating their mindless, brutal violence that resolves nothing. Damn them all to hell."

"Nothing is that absolute," said Cody.

Denise gave the boy in her lap a hug.

"I'm been raising this little one to be different." She placed another kiss on the tousled head of hair. "Or at least I had been raising him that way until this happened. I'm a poet, you know. Ahmed has artistic talent. We'd created a lovely little world for our beautiful family. And all of a sudden it's gone. Ruined by violence."

"Mrs. Rashid," said Cody, "there's far more to this than that."

She said, "And I have been contaminated. I can't believe what I've done. I killed a man."

"You're going through hell," said Cody. "Anyone can see that. But trust me, ma'am, you're going from victim to victor. Don't give up now."

"It's not as simple as that," she said, "and you know it. What drives a man like you to embrace violence?"

Cody said, "Trouble."

At first she thought his one-word reply was his response. She realized that wasn't the case when she saw what Cody saw.

Headlights a half-mile down the road. A motorized caravan was advancing at a steady clip.

"Military convoy," growled Cody.

He immediately wheeled the side-by-side off the road, onto the rough desert ground at high speed distance from the highway and avoid the oncoming convoy. Even with the advantage of NVD, it was a rock 'n' roll ride, the side-by-side pitching and bucking without slacking speed.

When they were well away from the highway, Cody braked and killed the engine.

A handful of minutes passed. Then a Russian convoy passed

them in the near distance, thundering by without becoming aware of the side-by-side in the darkness. A command car was followed by troop transports and a pair of armored vehicles. Then they were gone on down the highway, tail lights eventually vanishing into the gloomy distance.

And so, hoped Cody, was Denise Rashid's conversation about man and his violence. Cody had his point of view, as any thinking person would, but he saw little value in speaking his thoughts on the subject to a woman who already had far more than enough to deal with.

Cody's philosophy? He did not consider himself a metaphysician, but experience had taught him that violence was as much a part of human nature as kindness; that combat was as much ingrained in the collective psyche as lovemaking. It's a crazy mixed-up world and a big part of that is every person on the planet processing data in their own way.

Fact of the matter: it's a violent world.

But no way does that fact negate or counter the abundant goodness of life. It was the Zen Buddhist Shaolin monks of ancient China who first developed the concept and refined the practice of kung Fu, for example, it being understood that the garden of contemplation *must* be defended against barbarians at the gate. Avoid physical confrontation, violence, whenever possible. If physical conflict is necessary, use your opponents' strength and energy against them. Simple as that.

More than an ancient metaphor or discipline, the concept is applicable to daily life in any context. One sees the decent, the defenseless, being discriminated against, abused, victimized?

Could be a person. Could be a country. Could be a way of life or someone you love. Your responsibility is to step in. Do something about it if you can. Defend. Protect.

And throughout history, unfortunately, doing so did require the use of force; of violence. One could hardly allow the barbarians to trample and destroy the garden that civilized humanity had so naturally and lovingly cultivated. Such is the role of violence in contributing to cleansing the planet of human nature's dark side; protecting, defending and facilitating a planet's collective human energy in its quest to survive.

Such was the way of life as Cody understood it.

The convoy rolled past, its taillights and rumbling racket reduced to diminishing red pinpoints in the distance, and then vanishing. Complete and total silence reclaimed the desert.

Was the convoy on its way to investigate the fighting at the oasis? Or were they repositioning with regard to whatever was going on at the American base in Syria? And did it really matter anyway? With Russia, the US, Iran and ISIS all with an interest in its outcome, Syria's civil war between the government and the FSA had become a bona fide free-for-all.

The only thing that really mattered about the convoy was that it was good and gone, headed off in the opposite direction. The night was again an uninhabited place except for the three people in the side-by-side.

No one had said anything during their wait for the convoy to pass. Ali remained silent on his mother's lap, securely held. His eyes remained open, missing nothing. Denise spent her time observing Cody and thinking.

Now she said, "Will there be more of them?"

"We'll soon find out," said Cody.

He reached for the ignition.

The extended silence had served in its own way to restore Denise's mental equilibrium. It had served her well, venting thoughts and emotions to this man, Cody. Now for sure he knew how he she felt. And after his reaction to the potential danger, avoiding the passing convoy just now, Denise realized that she was and Ali were safe in his hands. Cody was a man who *did* things. He only spoke when he felt like it. A man of action.

True, he was a man of violence. But he was a fine, *good* man who could only be judged by his actions as a man on the side of good; a man with God on his side. Considering how brutal and violent the world was showing itself to be could be, Ali growing up to be a man like Cody would be a good thing.

When she had the opportunity, Denise decided, she would let Cody know her gratitude for everything he was doing; her gratitude for being the man he was. For herself and Ali, he was the best chance they had.

The side-by-side fired up. It sounded terribly loud to Denise but she told herself it was okay. There was no one around to hear and, really, out here in the middle of nowhere, what choice did they have?

Cody kept the headlights off, continuing to depend on the NVD for safety sake. He brought the vehicle around and gave it some gas, heading in the direction of the highway.

That's when the left front tire hit a low pointy rock formation that really hadn't looked like much in the monitor. But it sure as hell was enough to send the side-by-side into a near flip, avoided only by Cody's expertise as a wheelman in braking and working the steering wheel with enough skill to bring them to an abrupt stop.

Something was definitely wrong with the front end.

"You okay?" he asked Denise.

She was hugging Ali closer than before.

"Yes, thank you. About what I said, Cody. It's how I feel…but I also know that if we survive this, it will be because of you."

Cody said, "Let me check the damage."

He got out of the side-by-side. He knelt down at the front end for a look.

The axle had neatly snapped in two.

They were stranded.

CHAPTER THIRTY

He heard the chopper before he saw it—a Boeing Apache AH-64 gunship. If one had served in a combat theater anywhere in the world during the past decade or more, they knew that sound. The Apache AH-64 is an American attack helicopter equipped with a nose-mounted sensor suite for target acquisition and a night vision system. It's armed with a 30mm chain gun carried between the main landing gear, under the aircraft's forward fuselage, and four mounted stub-wing pylons for carrying armament and storing missiles and rockets.

It appeared from the red dawn like some bloated prehistoric bird emerging from the fires of creation, its great rotor blades making an unmistakable sound not unlike a chainsaw backed by thunder.

These skies were heavily patrolled by both the Americans and the Russians. Cody had had the passing thought something like this could happen. But still it was almost too good to be true.

At first sight of the approaching helo, Denise stirred with a sharp jolt of something she could not at first identify. Joy and anticipation, emotions she hadn't felt in a while. A helicopter coming for them! She didn't know *how* and she didn't know *why* but when she saw that chopper, her heart took flight.

Next to her, Ali simply observed.

Cody was unsure why his relief was mixed with caution.

He reached into the side-by-side and retrieved the M4. An elusive mental gremlin was bugging the edge of his thoughts. He couldn't quite identify it. So much had been happening so fast. Yet the gremlin was telling him that something had been said in the recent past that he needed to remember. And he should remember it *now*. It was irritating as hell.

He became aware of Denise Rashid murmuring something beside him. He leaned in slightly to listen closer through the noise of the approaching gunship. She wasn't speaking to him. She was giving praise to God with her every breath.

Cody watched the chopper's approach with narrowed eyes. His mind kept trying to give that mental gremlin a name.

He told Denise, "You and the boy stay close to me."

"They're coming for us!" she gushed. "Oh glory be and praise the Lord! They've come to take us home!"

The gunship banked in to touch down in the dawn's early light, the chopper vanishing momentarily behind a veil of red dust, a sand storm kicked up by the rotors' backwash. The pilot made a wobbly landing. The pilot was either injured or an amateur.

Amateur.

The gremlin in Cody's mind got a name. And a swift kick in the ass. Captain Larson had referred to a missing US gunship.

Could this gunship be *that* gunship?

The pilot downshifted to idle. The rotors ceased their racket.

Denise broke away from Cody and went running toward the chopper before the dust had settled, her son's little hand in hers. Ali had no difficulty in keeping up. She moved so fast, Cody was caught off-guard. She was beyond his reach before he could stop her.

"Denise, *no!*"

She pretended not to hear him. Her mind was racing faster than it ever had with a joy that almost made her swoon.

Their transportation home! It truly was a new day! By tonight she and Ali would be in Rome with Ahmed. Their little family would be together again! Oh, yes yes yes! Thank you, Lord. Where was the pilot? She would give him a big hug with all the joy she felt. Glory be, they were going home!

The two-man crew emerged from the cockpit.

They were not in uniform. The pilot held a pistol, his copilot held a Russian AK-47 assault rifle. Their feet touched ground just as Denise and the boy reached the gunship.

Denise drew up at the sight of their drawn weapons, their shabby civilian clothes and their unkempt, bearded Arabic features. She hesitated, starting to turn back in Cody's direction, not releasing Ali's hand.

Her reaction was not fast enough.

Cody raised the M4, holding his fire with his finger on the trigger. The flurry of movement around the gunship made it impossible for him to draw bead on the two men without risking hitting Denise. Then it was too late anyway.

The pilot grabbed Denise's arm and roughly pitched her to the second man, who slung his rifle over his shoulder to catch her, taking firm hold of the woman by standing behind her, his fists holding her arms in his vise-like grip. Ignoring the boy, the pilot pressed the muzzle of his pistol against Denise's right temple.

The nineteen-year-old's name was Abdullah. His partner, Omar, was a year older. They were orphans of war. Eyes glittering with mad religious fervor.

Abdullah said, "Drop your weapon, American, or the woman dies."

Cody had hardly expected this mission to be a cakewalk but it was starting to seem as if every time they were close to breaking free, something like this happened. Less than an hour ago, Denise and Ali huddled nearby, he took on the guy blocking their way at the oasis. This time there was no way Cody could close enough in physically without harm befalling the hostages.

He set the carbine down at his feet. He said, "Who am I talking to?"

The pilot sneered.

"I am Abdullah." With mock civility, he lifted a hand to indicate his copilot. "Allow me to introduce Omar. But you see, you hardly need to know our names. We are your death, infidel. There is no God but Allah and we serve Him."

Well shit, thought Cody.

These guys were ISIS. Craziest of the crazies.

In a region overrun with warring parties, at least most of them had a practical motive and objective behind what they were fighting for: overthrow the government, defeat the rebels.

The US and Russia backing opposite sides for their own best interests.

But ISIS? Crazy as a soup sandwich. Their only goal was the foundation of an Islamic state; specifically, a caliphate, meaning an Islamic State led by a single group of religious authorities under a supreme leader who is believed to be descended from the Prophet Mohammed.

Cody reminded himself that there was one similarity to that earlier face-off at the oasis. You could never tell what was going to happen next in a wild card situation like this with guns and stupidity involved. As long as he could keep this sneering terrorist talking, there was the possibility of turning this thing around.

Cody indicated the gunship. "Nice ride you boys have got."

Abdullah's sneer grew wider. "The Russians taught me how to fly when I was in Hezbollah. Now I am ISIS." He chuckled without humor. "And I still know how to fly."

"How'd you get your hands on it? That is, if you don't mind me asking."

Cody intended to work this fool. The guy had an ego big as a house. Cody was as skilled in field interrogation as he was in interrogation room settings back home. Both involved a quick read of the personality being dealt with, and then proceeding accordingly. Call it playing mind games. Cody was a master of that game.

Any chance of turning this around would rest on playing this man who stood holding a gun to the head of the woman. This ISIS fanatic's fiery spirit was a strength built on ego. He was likely high on something in addition to his fanaticism:

speed, hashish, who knew? But this resulted in him being far more focused on his own bullshit than he was on the reality of the moment. He hadn't even instructed Cody to unleather the Glock holstered at his hip. Egotists love to brag. Cody hoped to use this ISIS fanatic's strength against him as surely as if they were engaged in physical combat.

The terrorist snarled, "ISIS takes what we need. This helicopter was there for the taking."

"Easy as that, eh?"

"The pilots were young and foolish. Easy to kill."

"Care to tell me about it?"

Cody worked at masking the revulsion that coursed through him. He spoke as if he wasn't addressing a man who was holding a gun to a woman's head.

"It was child's play," sneered Abdullah. "Literally child's play. Two of our women. Three of our children. We concealed ourselves as they waved down the chopper."

"Those pilots had protocol," said Cody. "They shouldn't have landed."

"It was a convincing performance," countered Abdullah with a smirk. "An overturned vehicle. Two women, three children in the middle of the road, waving desperately for assistance. You American males consider yourselves so heroic, do you not? John Wayne. Clint Eastwood. You cannot let the helpless go unheeded. And so the young heroic pilots landed this gunship. We killed the pilots and have been flying merrily about the countryside ever since, delivering Allah's vengeance to the infidels. Does that anger you, American?"

"You know it does," said Cody.

"Good. You will die knowing that after you are gone, ISIS will continue to seize land and take over the entire earth until our blessed flag covers all of the east and west, to every last extent of the earth. We will conquer the world! All religions who agree with democracy must die!" Abdullah was spraying spittle now as his fervor intensified. "You shall not live to see it, American, but mark these words. ISIS shall never stop growing and spreading. We will strike a never ending war against the Crusader-Zionist enemy in every place in the world!"

While this conversation was taking place, while Omar maintained his steely grip of Denise's arms and Denise strained against the imprisoning hold...no one was paying attention to the ten-year-old boy.

But Ali was paying close and careful attention to every word and every move of these adults towering over him. He mainly kept shifting his attention between Abdullah and Omar before making his decision. Both men posed an immediate danger to his mother, Omar holding her still while Abdullah pressed the pistol to her temple. Ali reasoned that if his mom was unhindered, they would stand a better chance.

With that decision made, Ali reached down unobtrusively to lift the hem of his frock just enough for him to wrap his fist around the handle of the knife hidden there. Ali drew the knife without anyone noticing. Then, using both hands, he rammed the knife with all his strength into the outside upper thigh of the man holding his mom.

Omar roared his pain like a wounded bear.

Several things happened simultaneously. Omar's first automatic reflex, after lifting his voice in agony, was to thoughtlessly release his hold on Denise. The movement of his arms, lowering toward the knife buried to its handle in his flesh, knocked aside Abdullah's pistol from the side of Denise's head. Without a second's hesitation, Denise grabbed Ali's little hand and they started running away.

Cody was unlimbering the Glock from its holster. Planting his feet squarely and with a two-handed grip, he centered his bead on Abdullah who was lowering his gun into target acquisition after it having been knocked aside. Cody carefully squeezed the Glock's trigger.

And not a damn thing happened.

His gun had jammed!

With Omar on his butt, growling rather than howling his pain, Abdullah triggered a round that kicked up dirt directly in front of the running woman and her child. As intended, this drew Denise up sharply without her releasing the boy's hand. She turned to see Abdullah again pointing his pistol at her, this time from a distance but with the same steady aim.

"Go no further," he commanded. "Return to me."

Denise glanced in Cody's direction.

This man who had come so close to saving her and her son now stood like a statue. The M4 carbine remained near his feet but he was making no move for it. His eyes were on the gun in Abdullah's hand, aimed at her.

Cody knew that if he made any move for the carbine, Abdullah would pull the trigger and she would be dead. Bringing her and Ali home safely was his mission, not throwing away her life to get his hands on a weapon. He looked like a panther about to pounce into action but for this fragment of time, he was biding his time.

With a haunted, conquered look returning to her eyes and demeanor, Denise started walking back toward the men from ISIS. This time she did not have the heart to lead the boy by the hand but he stayed close to her side.

Omar freed the knife blade from his flesh with a single mighty tug that resulted in a string of filthy curses, then he was back up on his feet, his ferocious growl sounding like an angry bear. Omar was a seasoned street fighter way before he'd become a terrorist. He'd evolved into a hardened desert fighter in the service of his god. He was now aroused with insane bloodlust. His eyes fastened on the woman and the child, both of whom drew up short when they realized he was advancing on them. He was now holding the knife in his right hand. His own blood dripped from its blade. There was murder in Omar's eyes.

He reached out with his huge left hand to grab Ali. "I will kill them both!" he screamed. "And the boy dies first!"

CHAPTER THIRTY-ONE

Cody wasn't about to save his own life by allowing a child to be murdered. He made his move, fast, for the M4 on the ground. In this crazy, tumbling instant there was enough going on downrange, the other players all too involved in their own drama, for anyone to notice him grabbing hold of the carbine.

Omar had almost reached the boy, his left arm reaching out to grab the Ali by the throat while raising his right hand to bring the blade down. Denise was screaming frantically for him to stop, throwing herself in front of her son to ward off Omar with both hands, begging him to show mercy.

Abdullah was shouting at Omar. "Kill the boy! Not the woman! Not the woman," Abdullah kept repeating. He still holding the pistol in his right hand, reaching with his free hand to grasp Denise by one of her arms, dragging her from the path of Omar's raised knife.

Abdullah had his own agenda and with that act, Cody made sense of it. Sex trafficking was common in this part of the world where powerful, corrupt, untouchable men of the upper crust—

oil sheiks and the like—were still known to maintain captive harems. In a world such as that, a white woman of Denise's class would be worth a king's ransom.

While the tumultuous scene played out, Cody brought up the M4 undetected. He would take out Omar first, of course. Because of Denise's resistance, Abdullah's response would be delayed and that would buy enough time for Cody to plant a bullet right between the Abdullah's eyes.

And then something rather extraordinary happened.

Omar's head exploded.

One second there was the murderous, hate filled-face full of nothing but aggression. Next instant the man's entire head silently blew apart in a violent, messy splatter of skull fragments, body fluids and brains. Without a head, he stood there for several seconds as if not sure what to do next. Then Omar's knees buckled and his headless corpse toppled to the ground. The knife dropped from lifeless fingers.

A heartbeat later everyone heard the report of the rifle shot from the distance as the speed of sound caught up with the bullet; a battlefield phenomenon Cody had witnessed more than once.

Then came the approaching sound of thundering hoof beats.

Cody tracked the carbine's muzzle on Abdullah who, in response to what happened to Omar, had momentarily forgotten about Denise and Ali. He stared down at the remains of his companion. He then whirled in the direction of the oncoming hoof beats that had materialized into galloping horses rushing onto the scene.

It was like being in the middle of a stampede. The blinding cloud of red dust was again kicked up, this time by the pounding hooves of horses. The dancing clouds of dust obscured Abdullah as well as the features of the hard-riding horsemen who came swooping in.

Denise Rashid and her little boy emerged from the roiling mini dust storm. Cody, holding the M4 with its butt against his right hip and his finger curled around the trigger, scooped up the boy so that Cody's body served to partly shield Ali. Denise Rashid drew close as she could to Cody. She was whispering words of encouragement in her son's ear.

The dust finally cleared.

Cody was not that surprised to see Zahran, mounted in all his supreme glory atop a white Arabian charger that trotted over.

The Syrian appeared no different from earlier when he'd intercepted Cody's team on their way to the oasis. His Stetson rode proudly atop his head held erect while his smartly tailored western duds still made him appear far more like stand-in for Tom Selleck in a cowboy movie than the desert warlord he was. The assault rifle he held, now aimed skyward, only added to the impression.

He seemed to be having a grand time.

"Ah, my American friend!" The hearty, booming greeting was delivered as if to a long lost dear friend in a good time nightspot. "And where are your FSA companions, partner?"

"Fortunes of war," said Cody.

That was enough from one combatant to another.

Zahran observed the woman and child. "I see your mission

was a success." He nodded with a tip of his Stetson to Denise. "Do not worry, little lady. No harm will come to you while you are in my domain. And you see," he chuckled with a wide sweep of an arm, "it is all my domain."

Zahran shook a cigarette loose from his pack of Marlboro's and fired it up.

The world had quieted down around them. With the dust settled, Cody saw that next to where Omar lay, a horseman stood pointing a rifle at Abdullah. The terrorist's burning scowl remained hateful. He was not happy in custody.

Cody set Ali down, expecting the boy to rejoin his mother, but Ali had something else on his mind. He went to where the knife lay upon the ground near the headless, much bloodied remains of Omar. Flies were already gathering and feasting around the gaping cavity of red muck between the cadaver's shoulders.

Ali reached down, intending to callously clean off the knife blade on Omar's clothing. He changed his mind when he saw up close how messy with gore the clothes were. Instead he sunk the knife blade into the desert sand. He appeared to handle the knife with a degree of familiarity. When he withdrew the blade, the abrasive sand had dry cleansed it of blood. Ali returned the knife to its hiding place at his calf beneath the frock he wore.

Zahran observed this, nodding his approval. "The boy learns fast, I see. This ordeal he now suffers through will serve him well as he becomes a man."

Denise took exception to this with a pained expression. "No, he is my little baby. How can you be proud of what you see? The boy is only ten years old!"

"I killed my first man when I was twelve," said Zahran. He flipped away his half-smoked Marlboro. "In the desert, a child becomes a man very quickly."

"Then I shall take him home and never let him see a desert again," said Denise with her chin up, maybe in shock but still ready to take on one and all. "Dear God, let there still be a place in this world for innocence."

"Not here," Zahran said with a nod to indicate Omar's body. "Not here."

Ali again stood at his mother's right. Denise Rashid's right arm was draped across his shoulders, an endearing embrace that held her him near.

Cody returned his attention to the faux American cowboy towering over him on the white horse. He said, "Thanks for taking a hand. Sure was looking bad until you stepped in."

Zahran flashed his friendly, ear to ear smile. "I did not 'step in,' amigo. I have been shadowing you since our last encounter."

"You could have pitched in at the oasis."

"That was not my fight."

"Well anyway I'm obliged to you for pitching in when you did. I'm glad this one was your fight, too."

"Of course it was. This is my range, partner. I do not abide rustlers riding my range." He made his point by spitting upon the remains of Omar, adding, "I have been at odds with ISIS rascals for some time. Everyone has, it seems. They have cost me men and revenue with their foolishness. Harmful foolishness. Troublemakers."

Cody had the impression Zahran would have spat again if he'd had phlegm to spare. Cody nodded in Abdullah's direction.

"This one was bragging to me about them killing two American soldiers to gain possession of the gunship. What are your plans for him?"

"Nothing good," said Zahran. "We will hold him for questioning. I share what I learn with the Americans, by the way."

"You could turn him over to the US military for interrogation."

Zahran left the saddle. He stood face to face with Cody. "I think not," he countered mildly. "Our means of extracting information are," he paused in difference to Denise's presence, searching for the right word. He finished with, "...our means are more effective, let us say. It will not end well for that one." He extended his pack of Marlboro's to Cody with a practiced flick of the wrist. "Have a smoke?" he offered.

"No thanks. I hear they're not good for your health."

A gentle jibe that made Zahran chuckle. "In this part of the world, my friend, just *living* can be bad for your health. Our prisoner will find that out the hard way, I promise you."

Denise Rashid said, "I'd like a cigarette, please."

Zahran's manner softened. "But of course, dear lady."

She extracted a cigarette from the pack he extended to her. He lit her cigarette. Denise puffed nervously, staring off into the distance at nothing. Saying nothing.

Cody told Zahran, "I've lost radio contact with Deir ez-Zour."

The warlord frowned. "That's off my range. Other side of the river. I don't cross the river and everyone on the other side leaves me alone. Good politics, you see. But word has reached me of much fighting over there. Many dead, I have heard. Early reports, they are always sketchy, is that not so? Much is happening tonight, eh?"

Before Cody could respond, there was a sharp cry of pain from nearby.

Everyone brought their eyes around in that direction just in time to see the rider, who had been standing guard over Abdullah, fall to his knees and then onto his side, then onto his back. The blade of a knife had been rammed to the hilt into his heart.

Abdullah ran to leap astride the murdered rider's horse. He swung the mount about and took off with the horse at full gallop.

Zahran's remaining riders started to give chase. Zahran lifted a hand that brought them to a stop.

Cody said, "I hope you're not letting that son of a bitch get away."

"Hardly," said Zahran. "We are men of honor, are we not, Cody? It is you who must deliver justice to the jackal. Although it would be nice if you brought him back alive." The warlord extended to Cody the reins of the white charger. He said, "Be my guest."

Cody wanted to jump into that saddle immediately. Everything in him wanted to give chase. But the mission was not about tracking down ISIS members.

He glanced questioningly at Denise.

She threw away her cigarette. Her face was an angry mask. She said, "That son of a bitch tried to kill my son."

That was good enough for Cody.

He leapt into the saddle.

CHAPTER THIRTY-TWO

The last thing Cody heard before becoming enveloped by the pounding of the white stallion's hooves was the warlord, Zahran, shouting after him. "Ride 'em, cowboy! Hi-yo Silver, away!"

The guy was cheering Cody on as if from the stands at some horse race.

But this was no for fun and games.

Cody was bent over low in the saddle, stroking the stallion's snow white mane, whispering encouragement into the horse's ear. It figured that a warlord would have himself a horse that could eat up distance. That was a blessing now considering Abdullah's head start.

Cody was yielding to impulse, something he generally avoided doing in dangerous situations. But in this case the impulse was damn worthy. Zahran and his men could easily have given chase. A round from Cody's Glock would have ended it if the Glock wasn't jammed. And the warlord was right. This *was* personal. Cody had killed tonight during the rescue of the hostages. That was his mission; his job. But this scumbag Abdullah, who he was now in pursuit of, was in a whole other league.

Personal, yeah.

Hijacking an American gunship. Slaughtering its crew. Leaving their remains for the vultures and jackals somewhere in a trackless desert. Abdullah had the blood of those American servicemen on his hands and God only knew what other atrocities. Cody wasn't about to let him get away.

The trail started to climb, continuing to rise sharply until abruptly flattening out into a tabletop mesa. If Abdullah held his lead and made it that far he might have a chance of escape across the open desert no matter how good a horse Cody's stallion happened to be. Abdullah became only vaguely visible on the trail ahead because of the cloud of dust he was leaving in his wake.

Cody kept whispering to his horse. "That's it, big fella. Close the distance. Let's get 'em."

The Arabian steed likely recognized English commands since his master was the western lingo-spouting Zahran. But the horse got the idea.

Cody began gaining as the trail grew even steeper, racing past ancient trees, some towering fifty feet high; long since reduced by the elements to little more than pointy towers of dead wood rooted deeply into the desert floor, lining the dusty trail like giant sentinels along the steep rise leading up to the plateau. Cody was now closing in enough to clearly make out Abdullah up ahead, furiously whipping his horse to coax from it more speed.

Cody whispered, "That's it, boy. Just a little more now. Right! We've got 'em!"

They gained the plateau together, their horses hurtling along now side by side at high speed. Cody launched himself from his saddle, sailing into Abdullah. They toppled from the horses and went sprawling to the ground.

Cody was first to regain his footing.

Abdullah stood, his haughty demeanor gone. He was disheveled. Out of breath. Standing with his back only inches from the precipice of a cliff. He realized his precarious position but Cody gave him no time to react.

Cody said, "Tell everyone in hell I said hello."

He crossed a right to Abdullah's chin. The blow knocked the terrorist back on his heels. Cody followed through by popping him with a left, then stabbing another left to the mouth, finishing with a hard right cross. He would always remember the venomous hissing Abdullah made when he went over.

The hissing ceased abruptly, interrupted by a strange skewering sound.

Cody went to the lip of the precipice. He peered over the edge.

Abdullah's body was impaled on the tallest dead tree at the base of the cliff.

Cody returned to the others a few minutes later. He led the horse Abdullah had stolen to make his escape. He handed the reins to one of Zahran's horsemen. Before dismounting from the white stallion, he made a brief study of those he'd left behind minutes earlier.

Zahran and Denise Rashid were engaged in conversation. They paused when Cody arrived. Apparently the warlord had just said something amusing. Denise appeared battered with grime and fatigue. But it did Cody good to see her registering the briefest, pretty little smile at whatever Zahran had said. The Iraqi cowboy appeared to exert a calming influence on her.

Ali continued to watch everything with eyes wide and his little mouth zipped shut. But there was a subtle change there also. The boy's staring, appraising eyes, seeming never to blink, continued to carefully study Cody's every move and manner—a boy scrutinizing the world and ways of men. But those gazing eyes were no longer tinged with fear, studying Cody with unabashed awe.

Cody dismounted. He handed Zahran the reins.

"Thank you."

The warlord looked like a man who'd just won a high stakes horse race. "Hey amigo, what are friends for, eh? You left him for us?"

"If you want him. I left him for the jackals and the vultures."

"You're sure he was dead when you rode away?"

"Dead as they come," Cody assured him. Tired as he was, he found himself smiling with genuine relief at the relaxed expression worn by Mrs. Rashid. Cody added, "I see you two are getting acquainted."

Denise regarded Zahran with open admiration in her eyes and voice. "How can such a considerate, amusing man to be called a warlord?"

"Ask Omar," said Cody with a nod at the headless remains nearby.

Cody shared her admiration and appreciation of the warlord. He liked the guy, too. But Cody hadn't come all this way to make friends. And he couldn't get Sara and the battle at Deir ez-Zour out of his mind.

Zahran seemed to read him perfectly. He said, "My men and I will escort you three to the river. From there it is not far to the base."

Cody's eyes were on the helicopter. He said, "Appreciate the offer, pard. But right now we're burning daylight."

Zahran frowned. "Burning daylight?"

"Wasting time. I want to get these two," Cody indicated Denise and Ali, "back to Deir ez-Zour ASAP."

Zahran's exuberance beamed with a new addition to his vocabulary. "Burning daylight," he said. "ASAP. But, amigo—"

"No buts. No time." Cody gestured for the woman and her son to join him. "Right now it's airpower we need, not horsepower."

"A noble aspiration," said Zahran, "but of all I have to offer, sadly I have no man to pilot this chopper. Where would we find such a man?"

Through it all, the Apache AH-64 had remained on low idle; rotors unmoving, the low muted *thrummmm* of its turbine engine audible only because all the excitement had died down.

Cody said, "I may be rusty but I have been trained and I have experience."

Zahran kept right on beaming. "But of course you do. I

should have known. A noble aspiration meets the man who is nobility itself!"

"Let's not overdo it," said Cody.

The woman and child had joined them. Cody led them around to the side of the chopper. Zahran kept pace.

"I overdo nothing," said the warlord. "You bested me in our match of fisticuffs." He glanced at Denise and confided, "No one on my range as ever done that. At least, none who lived long to brag about it."

Denise paused to gaze up at the gunship; an impressive weapon of death and destruction towering over them, already warm to the touch in the early morning sunshine.

Zahran said Denise with a broad, gallant bow, pretending to be crestfallen, "You leave me behind to cherish this memory of our meeting forever, madam."

Denise acknowledged the remark with the briefest smile, it being apparent in her eyes that she now had only one thing on her mind. She turned her hopeful eyes to Cody.

"You can get us away from here? If only this nightmare would end! My dear husband must be so worried about us. He'll glad to see us."

Cody went about assisting Denise and her small son into the copilot cockpit behind his own. Denise followed his suggestions in boarding and donned the flight helmet that should allow them to communicate during flight. Her son showed no hesitation and soon was strapped in seated on his mother's lap; a somewhat cumbersome arrangement, but one that would keep the boy safe.

Cody set up Denise up with a set of earphones so they could communicate in flight if necessary.

Despite the boy's withdrawn attitude, Cody realized how memorable this experience would be for a ten-year-old. He had a momentary flashback of his own kids when he reached out to ruffle the boy's already unkempt hair in an effort to instill some positive energy in the child.

"Ready for a chopper ride, Ali?"

No response. Eyes wide. Interested. But Ali Rashid stared only straight ahead without comment.

Denise caught Cody's eye before he lowered and clamped shut their canopy. She said, "Thank you, Mr. Cody. My son and I owe you our lives. I know we are in good hands. God bless you."

"We could all use a dose of good blessing," said Cody. "See you two in Deir ez-Zour."

Moments later, he was strapped into the cockpit, familiarizing himself with the impressive array of controls before him.

He was doing his best to recall startup procedure when Zahran stuck his head into the cockpit, marveling at the array of gauges, switches, and gadgets. Cody liked this galoot who had somehow managed to be born a Middle Eastern sheik. But two noncombatants aboard and Sara fighting without him in Syria meant it was time to get gone.

Zahran eyed one of the gauges. "Will you have enough fuel to reach your base?"

Cody had only a second before snapping the canopy cockpit canopy shut, blocking the warlord out. He said, "Let's find out."

CHAPTER THIRTY-THREE

At first the takeoff was shaky, not too unlike Abdullah's crappy landing, but within minutes it all came back to Cody, much like riding a bicycle; rusty at first, maybe, but there are some ingrained procedures, once learned, that you never forget. Cody had full control of the chopper by the time the warlord and his band on the ground had dwindled away in the chopper's backwash to become dots in the distance before vanishing from sight altogether.

Cody's last view of Zahran was the cowboy sheik using his white Stetson in one hand, sending them off with expansive waves. Despite everything, Cody couldn't help but chuckle.

They were soon on course, making good time. It was a fine day for flying, a beautiful, cloudless day. Sunlight sparkled off the Apache's cockpit canopy. Below, the desert was flat, extending forever in every direction. It didn't take long for Cody to begin feeling almost relaxed at the controls.

The flight sounds of the gunship surrounded him almost

like a cocoon. Its steady drone did not sooth his senses but rather honed them to a razor edge. He would not relax until they reached the US base in Syria and he found whatever would be waiting for him there.

But even with that factored into his mindset, truth was he'd been a pilot since his college days; since well before signing up for the military and his later government service. His dad, an Air Force pilot, had ingrained in Cody a love of flying, and once that bug bites, it never goes away.

There was no communication from Denise riding behind him. Cody could imagine she was trying to recharge herself as they flew along. If anyone deserved some rest, it was Mrs. Rashid and her little boy.

Cody was wide awake, his mind and reflexes working fine. He'd learned early on in his field work for the CIA that adrenaline was a field agent's best friend when a mission went hardscrabble as this one had.

It wasn't much of a flight time-wise.

Trouble came into view soon enough: the small US base carved out of the desert floor. The adjacent oil corporation facility with its nearby cluster of trailers and structures where the oil company personnel had resided. From this distance, the surrounding landscape reminded Cody of a field scene from back home; a broad swath of land scorched black after a controlled burn.

He saw no flares or flashes of combat. But *scorched* was the word, yeah. There had been a hell of a battle on this ground. The fact that fighting had ended had ended brought some relief.

But then there was the question: who made it through alive? Who survived?

Sara?

Cody worked the radio, not knowing what coded protocol to use and so simply broadcasting as the approaching view drew closer.

"Friendly and coming in," he said. "Do you copy? Apache gunship. Friendly. Coming in. Do you copy?"

No reply. Not even static.

* * * * *

The base comm shed had sustained only minor damage during the battle. Part of the roof was missing along with a minor section of one wall. Other than that, communications were again operational, full communication with the outside world having been restored once air cover intervened to turn the tide of battle.

Sara and Sergeant Samuels stood with Lieutenant Perez, the acting CO, observing a helicopter gunship advancing from about a mile out.

Perez was speaking into a handheld mic. "Identify yourself. This is a combat zone. You are intruding on American airspace. Identify and state your intentions."

Perez was in his late twenties. The grime of his uniform and smudged cheekbones bespoke heavy involvement in the fighting. Sara had long ago noted that island cultures bred strong men. The English. The Japanese. The Cubans. Many others.

Perez possessed the severe countenance of his race.

Samuels, who was the lieutenant's senior by about a dozen years, said in a mild voice, "Could be our missing gunship come home to roost."

"Then why aren't they identifying themselves?"

Sara said, "Radio trouble? You are going to let them touch down, right?"

Perez stared at the oncoming gunship with narrowed, steely eyes. "If that helo has been taken over by hostiles, I'm not about to let them blow up this base with one of our own rockets."

A gunnery sergeant hovered close by, awaiting the acting commander's next order.

Sara's stomach was balled into a tight knot of anxious uncertainty. She didn't know what to think and the uncertainty pissed her off. What if Perez was right? What if those were terrorists up in that chopper? Where the hell was Cody?

Perez spoke sharply into the mic.

"Identify. This is your last warning. You will be blown out of the sky if you do not identify yourself immediately. I repeat. Identify. This is your last warning."

* * * * *

Denise Rashid's voice crackled in the earpiece of Cody's flight helmet. She said, "Have you thought about giving it a kick?"

Distracted by everything he was seeing, doing and the frustration he was going through, Cody thought for a moment he'd misheard. "Excuse me?"

"It's not working, right? The radio, I mean. Shouldn't you be talking to them or something? I'm just saying a kick might help."

He was keeping everything straight in his mind. He did not wish to be impolite. He spoke gently as he could. "What are you talking about, Denise?"

"My grandpa used to be a TV repairman when I was a little girl," Denise said. "He'd let me go with him on house calls."

Cody said, "TV repairmen. House calls. Those were the days."

He was listening to her but his focus stayed on what he knew would be going on at that base without there being any radio communication between them. Did they think this gunship had been hijacked? Did they think he was about to open fire on them?

Denise was saying, "Grandpa told me that some models were so complicated he would just give them a good swift kick to make some connection pop somewhere in the wiring and get the set working again. All I'm saying, Mr. Cody, is that maybe you should try that now." Then she added in a small apologetic voice, "Of course, I don't know very much about jet airplanes."

A needle of sharp awareness pricked Cody's mind. If he could hear Denise, something *was* connecting somewhere inside the Apache's intricate communications wiring. They were about to be vaporized out of existence. But if he and Denise could communicate with each other inside the cockpit, was there hope?

What did he have to lose?

Cody drew back his knee and delivered a swift, short boot-kick to the console. Then he resumed speaking into the mic, trying not to rush his words because of the urgency of time slipping away.

He said, "Hold your fire! Friendly. Do you copy? I repeat, hold your fire. I'm bringing home a wounded bird."

When Sara heard Cody's voice coming across the speaker in the comm shed, a happy little shriek escaped from her not unlike a high school kid cheering her guy who just scored one the big game.

"Lieutenant," she said, "that's Cody! Hand me that mic."

The young lieutenant's prompt reflex was to obey the command of this woman from Washington.

Perez said, "I'm glad it ended this way," and he handed Sara the mic.

As her man brought in the Apache gunship in for a touch-down, Sara said into the mic, "Welcome home, soldier."

The landing went smoothly enough considering that it was the first helicopter landing performed by Cody in years. Within minutes the dust was settling, and Cody was initiating the chopper's shutdown procedure. The whirring of the rotors and the turbine drone faded into relative quiet.

Personnel were approaching at a scramble. Men toting fire-fighting equipment. Medical personnel.

Cody saw it all through eyes that were just now beginning to feel tired. Not too tired, though, to see Sara leading the pack toward him, glowing with the biggest smile Cody had ever seen.

EPILOGUE

President Harwood's expected "routine" press conference was anything but, thanks to a new set of fiery allegations aimed at his administration by the opposition party concerning shady campaign shenanigans during the previous election. POTUS's skill at thinking on his feet, and what he suspected were largely baseless allegations anyway, allowed him to get through the forty-minute ordeal. But by the time he left the podium, with calls of *"please, one more question, Mr. President!"* ringing in his ears, Martin Harwood felt like he'd been dragged behind a truck across a country mile.

Corbett was waiting offstage with the good news. "They made it, sir. Mrs. Rashid and her son are back under US protection."

Those few simple words sent Harwood's spirit soaring as nothing else could have. "Thank God. What about Sara and Cody?"

"Both doing okay."

The president paused where he and his Chief of Staff stood, momentarily aside from the post-press conference hubbub that circulated around them. He said, "And so the world is back on its axis. Jim, it almost felt apart on us over there in Syria."

Corbett nodded grimly. "The international diplomatic corps on both sides are going to have their work count out for them on this one."

"You've damn well got that right," said the president. His eyes were bleak. "At a time of high geopolitical tension, the military forces of one nuclear superpower directly engaged hundreds of heavily armed and hostile citizens of another superpower, who may or may not have been acting at the behest of that superpower."

Corbett said, "If we can maneuver through a mess like that, this latest domestic flimflam should be a walk in the park."

"And nothing more," Harwood agreed. "We do, after all, have the truth on our side."

"Along with God," Corbett commented with a small, wry smile." This could have had a better ending. Mr. Rashid's legacy will be the proof he brought over of what we've been up against for decades with Syria. This hostage rescue, when we do go public with it, will bring Rashid's death and what he did even more attention than before. Too damn bad we had to lose him, but his wife and son are on their way home. Word is Mrs. Rashid wants them streamlined straight back to the states."

"Can't blame her for that," grunted the president. "The United States of America can be one hell of crazy place. But it's no Syria."

Corbett drew a deep breath. "So it's back to work then. We'll need to come up with something to counter the mud the opposition is throwing at us."

"We will," said the president with quiet confidence. "The people of this country have their eye on us, Jim, and they'll never take it off. That's as it should be. The only thing I'd change is that we could reveal to America the whole story; that we could tell the citizens of this country how much they owe Sara Durell and Suicide Cody."

* * * * *

Deir ez-Zour Province—0700 hours

The RTL mercenaries had returned to collect their dead from the still smoldering battlefield. Cody and Sara found a spot to themselves from which to observe at the perimeter of the US base.

An oppressive quiet hung over the grisly scene beneath the lingering black cloud of smoke that did little to dissipate the rising desert heat. Sound carried clearly; weary men grunting their exertion as they loaded unrecognizable human remains onto waiting vehicles to be carted away.

Sara observed the carnage with grim, sad eyes. "RTL was in the wrong part of the world to try a simple mass assault on an American military position."

"Estimates are they lost some 500 men," said Cody. "I doubt anything this stupid and arrogant will be tried anytime soon."

A fresh US gunship had touched down to airlift Denise Rashid and Ali to Qatar. Mrs. Rashid's eyes stared only straight ahead as she went through the motions of boarding. One got the impression she was already gazing into a better future somewhere else. Back straight. Chin up. She'd make it.

The boy was sullen. In shock. Withdrawn. And yet Cody found reason to hope that, with enough love and guidance, Ali would grow out of this ordeal.

Also loaded aboard the outbound chopper were the remains of Captain Larson, the only American casualty. The young CO had gallantly sacrificed his life in defense of their position.

A silver lining in all of those clouds was the report that Lieutenant-Colonel Stratton and his copilot were safely back at the American airbase in Qatar. Their fighter jet had gone down in FSA-held territory where locals had gotten the pilots to safety for EVAC.

Cody had not gotten around yet to sharing the Zahran episodes with Sara, there was time enough for that. For now, he was just glad Stratton and his copilot had made it through the hellfire in Syria these past twenty-four hours.

So many had not.

There was the pair of heroic FSA militiamen, Yavuz and his buddy Arjan. No word yet had come in on Yavuz which could only mean both of those freedom fighters had gone down, consumed by the dogs of war. At least they were armed combatants who knew the odds going in.

Not so those more innocent souls: the kid, Aboo, who was man enough to fly a helicopter into a war zone from which he never returned. And his girlfriend, Aisha, a schoolgirl who took time from her studies to run what she thought was an innocent errand for her friends. Two souls of fresh, bright promise who no longer existed, savaged and destroyed by those same slavering dogs of war.

Such was the brutal reality of a civil war.

After some time, Sara drew her tired eyes away from the carnage. She said, "No one said this mission was going to be easy but dang, it sure got crazy in a hurry."

"Complicated," said Cody. "They're always complicated."

He was beginning to experience that subtle, gradual relaxation of body and spirit that came with the post-op wind-down phase of every mission.

He could see the same thing in Sara's eyes.

Sara said, "What's next, Cody?"

He slid his arm around her waist and drew her to him, Cody's first act of tenderness since he couldn't remember when. He said, "Our work here is done. We're catching the next flight out to Al Udeid."

She rested her head on his shoulder. "That sure enough sounds good to me, big guy."

Jack Cody exhaled a sigh that felt and sounded as if it came from somewhere down around his ankles. "I was hoping it would," he confessed. "I could use a break."

A LOOK AT: STONE
M.I.A. HUNTER BOOK ONE

A new kind of courage. A new kind of war.

Mark Stone has a score to settle. A former Green Beret, he has only one activity that gives meaning to his life - finding American's forgotten fighting men, the P.O.W.'s the government has conveniently labeled M.I.A.'s, and bringing them back from their hell on earth.

It's too big a job for one man. But Stone has friends. And with Hog Wiley and Terrance Loughlin-a merc from east Texas and a crack British commando - Stone returns to the steaming jungles of Laos on a do-or-die mission: to free a captured fighter jock from the sadistic commander who has sentenced him to a fate worse than death...

AVAILABLE NOW

ABOUT THE AUTHOR

Stephen Mertz is an American fiction author who is best known for his mainstream thrillers and novels of suspense. His work covers a wide variety of styles from paranormal dark suspense (Night Wind and Devil Creek) to historical speculative thrillers (Blood Red Sun) and hardboiled noir (Fade to Tomorrow). Mertz is also a popular lecturer on the craft of writing and has appeared as a guest speaker before writer's groups and at universities.

During high school and college, Steve regularly scandalized his "literary, well-intentioned" creative writing teachers with "thud and blunder melodramas." Throughout military service, travel, and a wide variety of jobs, his goal remained to become a publishing, full-time freelance professional. "It was never a question for me of if, but always when." His first national sale was to a mystery magazine, and his first novel, a detective thriller entitled Some Die Hard, was published under the pseudonym of Stephen Brett. Another Brett novel followed, as did a string of mystery and suspense short stories.